WE THE BEREAVED

WE THE BEREAVED

ANNA CLARKE

PUBLISHED FOR THE CRIME CLUB BY
DOUBLEDAY & COMPANY, INC.
GARDEN CITY, NEW YORK
1982

All the characters in this book
are fictitious, and any resemblance
to actual persons, living or dead,
is purely coincidental.

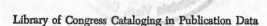

Library of Congress Cataloging in Publication Data

Clarke, Anna, 1919–
We the bereaved.

I. Title.
PR6053.L3248W4   1982   823'.914
ISBN 0-385-18359-3
Library of Congress Catalog Card Number 82-45539

WE THE BEREAVED

CHAPTER 1

As a solicitor, I occasionally have the depressing duty of visiting seriously ill or dying people in order to take instructions about the disposal of their wealth. Most of these clients are women, and usually, though not always, they have a lot of wealth to dispose of. The third factor that they often have in common is loneliness.

Miranda Porlock appeared from the file to be a typical case.

"Over to you, Harry," my junior partner had scrawled at the bottom of a telephone message. "Rich old girl about to snuff it. Jenny will give you the gen."

The neatly typed memo, clipped to the front of a file containing a few sheets of correspondence, stated that Miss Miranda Porlock, of Beth's Cottage, Mill Green, near Swanhurst, in Sussex, wanted urgently to make her will. At the moment, she was in an intensive care ward in the Queen Mary Hospital at Swanhurst, and according to the ward sister who made the telephone call, was not expected to last much longer.

I lifted my receiver and waited a few moments for Jenny—switchboard operator, receptionist, spare typist, general mainstay of the office—to find time to speak to me. My desk is in the bay window of the ground-floor room to the right of the front door, and I noticed that the shadow of the laburnum tree was long upon the grass. Office hours are from nine till five, and my partner and our small staff keep to them rigidly. They have homes and hobbies to go to. I have a three-bedroomed house that is so full of the memory of Imogen that I cannot bear to move from it. At the same time, returning to its emptiness after office hours becomes more and more of an ordeal every day, although it is over a year since she died.

In the office it feels bearable. We have the whole of a Victorian terraced house in a wide road near the centre of Swanhurst, a sleepy little town with a surprising amount of divorce work in addition to the bread-and-butter stuff of real and personal estate dealings. Geoff and I divide the work between us, each taking roughly the same number of similar cases, except that when a matter crops up late in the afternoon, as did Miranda Porlock's, Geoff leaves it to me, because he likes to get home to his wife and to their bridge evenings and he knows I don't mind working late.

"Sorry to keep you waiting, Mr. Johnson," said Jenny's voice in my ear. "I had a sudden rush of calls."

"Anything urgent?"

"Only this woman who's in hospital."

"Ah yes. That's what I wanted to know. Did they say when she could be visited?"

"As soon as possible. She's had a heart attack. They say her mind's quite clear, though," added Jenny, forestalling my next question.

"Porlock," I said. "It looks from the file as if she's consulted us once before. I suppose you don't remember her?"

"If she's the one I think she is, she's quite balmy."

"Most of our clients are."

"Well, yes, but even more so."

"In what way?"

I listened to the conscientious reply, and it suddenly occurred to me, first, that it was absurd to be having this long telephone conversation with somebody sitting in a room only a few yards away, and second, that Jenny must be longing to get away and I was keeping her by dragging out my questioning unnecessarily. She had two school-age children and a disabled husband. Her life was very tough and very full, but her overflowing compassion extended itself to her employer, who at sixty-two had health and wealth and good friends and a job he liked and nothing to complain about except that he had lost his wife over a year before.

Jenny knew that this was a bad time of day for me, particularly in this late-April sunshine, which picked out the worn patches of the wallpaper opposite my desk and threw its painfully clear light upon the summer days to come and upon all the years that lay ahead.

"I expect the old girl will want to leave her money to a cats' home," I said when Jenny had stopped talking.

She laughed dutifully and I had a sudden mental image of her telling her husband about poor Mr. Johnson, the lonely widower who didn't know what to do with himself after office hours, and what a pity

it was he didn't find himself another wife. The vision
angered me, and I said good night almost brusquely,
and told her not to wait any longer, since all the
others had gone and I would lock up the premises
myself.

A minute later I heard the front door bang. I was
alone in the house, and without any warning I was
attacked by a despair so monstrous that it took away
all powers of rational thought. My hands moved
about on the top of my desk. If there'd been a gun
lying there I'd have shot myself. But all I touched
was the thin folder containing last year's letter from
Miss Porlock asking for an appointment and the carbon copy of Geoff's reply.

I stared at the commonplace words and repeated
them in my mind as if they were some sort of magic
incantation that could save me from the pit of
blackness. Miss Porlock's letter was on a small piece
of a cheap brand of writing paper. It was short and
to the point.

"Dear Sirs, I need some legal advice and shall be
grateful if you will let me know when it will be con-
venient for you to receive a call. Yours truly."

The ink was black and the writing was small, firm,
and full of character.

"Dear Madam," I read from the blue flimsy paper
that we use for carbon copies of letters, "We thank
you for your communication of the 14th instant and
shall be happy to offer you our assistance. If you will
call at this office any afternoon next week between
two-thirty and three-thirty, the undersigned will be
glad to see you. Assuring you of our best attention,
yours faithfully, G. W. Holdsworth."

A harmless but rather oddly phrased letter, not Geoff's style at all. It must have been written and sent off by his secretary, Brenda, a competent but not always very tactful girl who liked to take things into her own hands, not always with happy results. There was nothing else in the file except Jenny's memo of today's date.

What had happened when Miss Porlock came to the office, and why had her business not been followed up? My mind worried at the little mystery, clinging to it as to a lifeline that might pull it out of its ocean of despair. Had we, as a law firm, failed her as a client? Certainly Geoff would have made a good enough impression. He always did. Young-looking middle-aged, a patient listener with a kindly manner that only those very close to him sometimes suspected was not entirely sincere; a clear and helpful adviser. Perhaps Brenda had given offence. Or perhaps it was simply one of those cases in which there is no follow-up, in which a client comes with a simple query, instantly answered, or with such preposterous proposals for litigation that any respectable solicitor has no alternative but to try to persuade them out of it.

One of your rich old girls. Geoff must have found out something about her in order to write that. I decided to telephone him. He would be home by now, and in any case he would be interested to know something about the case that had kept me in London for most of the day: an interminable war between divorced parents for the custody of a child, tragic in human terms but with considerable legal interest.

Jenny had left an outside line through to my extension. From Geoff's response I could tell that he and Sheila were enjoying their early-evening sherry and chat. I felt the sickening throb of envy and instantly quashed it. If I didn't snap out of this self-pity I might just as well go off and shoot myself. Get down to the business in hand: That was the only remedy. And also remember that even Geoff had his problems in the form of a nineteen-year-old son who would not stay at his university, would not get a job, and was constantly in some unsavoury sort of trouble. He also had a very satisfactory daughter with a nice husband and a nice home and a nice big mortgage and what would no doubt be a very nice grandchild now on the way, but shut up, Harry, you must not start comparing yourself with Geoff just now: You must get on with the job.

"Miranda Porlock," I said after telling him the latest on the custody case. "I'm just off to the hospital, but I see from the file that you've actually met her. Tricky one?"

"No madder than any of the others," said Geoff. "In fact rather shrewd, I'd say. Good brain gone to seed."

"But what did she want?"

"Oh some sort of—" Geoff broke off and over the wire I heard him call to his wife: "Shan't be a moment, darling, you can put the steaks in."

Again I quelled the envious flood.

"I can't remember too much about it," Geoff went on. "Some rigmarole about people spying on her . . . sounded rather like the usual paranoiac stuff."

I thanked him and hastily got off the line, wishing

I had not rung at all. Then I jumped up from my desk and began to collect a few papers, desperate to get out of the office before the blackness of mind should descend on me again. Over a year since Imogen died, and I seemed to be as bad as ever, with even the office no longer the refuge it had once been.

Miss Miranda Porlock is near to death and wants to make her will. It's your job to help her.

I repeated these words aloud to myself as I drove through the outskirts of Swanhurst towards the hospital, high on a hill with views of fine wooded countryside, but a cold and draughty spot for staff and visitors to get around in. The sun had gone in and a fine rain was falling. In the entrance hall I felt an animal relief at being warm and dry. The ward itself was actually much too hot. A tall, auburn-haired woman in a white coat introduced herself as Dr. Grace Watson.

"Harry Johnson," I said, shaking hands. "I got the message from my partner. How is Miss Porlock now?"

"Not too bad at the moment." The voice had a faint accent that I could not immediately place. Australian perhaps. "I know she wants to see you over a confidential matter," continued the doctor, "but I think it would be wise to have a nurse in attendance. Or I could stay myself if you'd prefer."

I looked into calm grey eyes that were on a level with my own and felt reassured, as if I had just escaped some very great danger.

"If you could spare the time," I said, "I do think that might be best. Sometimes these interviews can be difficult."

She smiled faintly. "That I can well believe."

"Is there anything I ought to know," I asked, "before we get going?"

"Try not to excite her. But you don't need telling that."

"I gather she has had a bad heart attack."

"That's only part of it," said the doctor. "We might have been able to cope with that, but she's also full of cancer—every vital organ. It's one of those strange cases where somebody carries on, apparently without too much pain or distress, until it's much too late to do anything. But it can't be very much longer now."

The grey eyes had suddenly flashed into life, and I thought: Ah, here are passion and compassion; I like Dr. Grace Watson.

She added, calmly again: "You'll want me to certify that she is mentally competent and can understand what she is doing?"

"Yes, please," I said.

The little side ward was crammed with oxygen cylinders and drip-stands and drainage tubes and all the other grisly paraphernalia for maintaining the heartbeat and the breath in a disintegrating human frame. The last thing that caught my eye was the occupant of the bed.

Wild-eyed and witchlike, Jenny had said, and wearing a sort of pink tea cosy for a hat.

But that had been some months previous. The face on the pillow looked to me more like a death mask, grey with a darker grey surround of coarse hair. Then the eyelids lifted and I could see at a glance both what Jenny had meant and what Geoff had meant by saying she was shrewd. The eyes were very dark and drugged and full of pain, but there was the light of intelligence there.

"Good evening, Miss Porlock," I said sitting down on the chair that Dr. Watson had placed for me. "I understand that you would like us to act for you in the matter of your will."

Very formal, but I've always found that this is the best policy on such an occasion.

The death mask with the living eyes made a slight movement and a faint voice said: "You are Mr. Johnson?"

"That's right."

"Harry Johnson? Is that your real name? Or is it Henry? And do you have another Christian name?"

"It's my real and only name," I replied, feeling rather surprised, because dying women do not usually waste their breath on such niceties. "My parents gave me no other."

"And you come from 4 St. Martin's Terrace, Swanhurst?"

"That's our office," I agreed.

Miss Porlock gave a little grunt as if of satisfaction and closed her eyes.

I glanced up at Dr. Watson, who was seated the other side of the bed. She laid a finger to her left temple and then gave a brisk nod, and I guessed that she was conveying to me her opinion that Miss Porlock's enquiries were intended to show that she knew exactly what she was doing and was perfectly capable of making her will.

That made sense, and I waited in silence for her to recover enough to go on.

"Can you draft the will for me to sign straight away?" she asked.

"Yes," I replied. "I've brought some standard forms in case one of them might suit you. If not, then perhaps you can dictate to me what you want done."

"I'll dictate it," she said. "It's very short."

She shut her eyes again and seemed to be summoning up her reserves of strength. The doctor and I again exchanged glances, and this time I did the nodding to show that all was going well so far. Then the low, breathless voice began to speak again.

"This is the last will and testament of me, Miranda Anne Porlock, of Beth's Cottage. . . ."

It took less than five minutes. She'd got it all perfectly correct; all the legal jargon, all the essentials were there. I wrote it in my rapid longhand and knew I should not need to alter a word. I was appointed as executor with authority to pay all costs out of the estate. There was only one clause: Her house and all its contents and everything else of which she died possessed were bequeathed to—

To whom?

At this point in the dictation the voice paused and I prompted her gently. For the first time since my arrival she appeared agitated, the dark eyes turning first towards the doctor and then to me.

"Would it be in order—" She broke off, gasped for breath, and began again. "Do you—as my executor—have to see the name of my beneficiary at this stage?"

In forty years of law practice I could not remember ever having been asked this question before.

"Well, it's usual," I said mildly. "After all, I shall have to know who to write to in the event of your decease, and since I am just about to make a fair copy of the document for you to sign in the presence of witnesses—"

"Oh, dear." The grey mask crumpled and tears showed in the eyes.

Dr. Watson signed to me. "Could you not leave a blank space," she said, "so that Miss Porlock can fill in the name and address, or names and addresses, herself?"

"Well, yes. I suppose I could do that."

Miranda Porlock smiled. The doctor and I stared at her. It was the most extraordinary sight. Not horrifying at all; in fact quite the opposite. The dark eyes sparkled and the wrinkles round the bloodless lips turned into laughter lines. The doctor and I gazed for a few seconds upon an expression of astonishing sweetness and warmth, an almost unearthly beauty. I am not a believing Christian, but at that moment I thought: Something has happened; the grace of God, if there is a God, has come to her and she is beyond pain and beyond human cares.

I looked up and saw from the expression on Dr. Watson's face that she felt the same as I did. But she must have been at many deathbeds, I thought: I wonder if she often sees this sort of thing.

I turned once more to the woman in the bed. "How much space do you want me to leave?"

She considered for a moment. "About two or three

lines. My writing does not take up much room, but I expect I shall have to sign or initial the insertion, shall I not, since it will appear in a different handwriting from the rest of the document."

I found myself laughing as I replied: "That seems a wise precaution."

Dr. Watson was smiling too. Whoever could have anticipated that a deathbed testament could turn into such a happy affair? I had never experienced anything like it, but happy, in a weird way, it certainly was, and it was Miss Porlock's doing. Or the doing of whatever spiritual force was moving through Miranda Porlock at this moment.

"You will be a witness to my signature, Doctor," she said when she had finished dictating and I was writing out the fair copy.

"Of course I will. And Mr. Johnson can be the other."

"No. Not Mr. Johnson. He has done enough. I would rather have one of the nurses."

"All right, my dear. Just as you wish."

I glanced up from my writing and saw that Dr. Watson was holding the patient's wrist. Good God, I thought, supposing she were to die now, just at this minute, before she can sign her will? What a horrible situation! Like Moses dying within sight of the Promised Land.

I finished my writing with a rush and waited in an agony of impatience while Dr. Watson rang for a nurse and propped the patient up against the pillows. When the ward sister arrived, they seemed to me to take an unconscionable time arranging Miss Porlock in a position in which she could write. I

knew it was absurd to feel like this. Miss Porlock was
just another client, nothing to me personally, and
even if she died before she had signed her will, I
would still have carried out my professional duties
faithfully and to the best of my ability.

Then, why was I tormenting myself with the sense
that I would have failed her? Was it just because I
had seen that astonishing look of peace and beauty
on her face that seemed to convey a benediction on
the two people—the doctor and the lawyer—who
were simply there to do their jobs?

At last they were ready and Miss Porlock asked
me for an envelope. I placed on the bed table the
long white envelope that I had brought with me and
laid beside it the paper on which I had been writing.
Dr. Watson held an arm round Miss Porlock's shoul-
ders, and the ward sister folded the sick woman's
fingers round a pen.

"Mr. Johnson," said Miss Porlock in a surprisingly
firm voice.

"Madam?"

"Would you please turn your back?"

"Certainly." I walked over to the window and
stared out at the darkening woods and hills. They
seemed to belong to another world, another life.
Imogen and I had spent many hours exploring this
countryside. Perhaps Miss Porlock had enjoyed walking too. And neither of them would ever see it again.

My eyes began to sting and the dark hill outline
began to blur. Had I been alone I would have paced
the room and wept and cried aloud. Over a year ago,
and the mourning was only just beginning, for this
was the first time I had felt the urge to weep beyond

all control. Or did this sense of utter abandon mean
that it was at last beginning to come to an end?

The voice with the faintly Australian accent came
to my ears.

"You can turn round now, Mr. Johnson. The operation is completed."

I blinked and hoped that the moistness in my eyes
did not show. The doctor and the ward sister were
standing either side of the bed, supporting the patient between them. Miranda Porlock held out the
long envelope to me. As I took it, her fingers
clutched at my sleeve and her eyes were beseeching.

"You won't open it—not till I'm dead?"

"I promise not to open it until the time comes, but
now that this business is finished I'm sure you will
feel better."

People are always a little superstitious about making their wills and they like to hear this conventional
little speech. It slipped out automatically, but in the
circumstances it was quite out of place. Miss Porlock
muttered something that could have been "thank
you," and then suddenly her mouth and eyes opened
wide and she gave a great cry.

"Help me!"

The ward sister bent over her and Dr. Watson
took me by the arm and led me to the door.

"Can I wait somewhere?" I murmured. "I'd like to
know how she is."

"In the out-patients waiting-room. There'll be no
one there. I'll be along as soon as I can."

"Thank you."

I put the big envelope in my briefcase and walked
along the passage to Out Patients, where I sat on a

hard bench and put my head in my hands and let the tears flow. There was no holding them back now. If Dr. Watson found me like this I didn't even care. I would not be the first to sit in a hospital corridor and howl my heart out.

But it was a long time before anybody came, and by then the flood had spent itself and I was slumped listlessly against the back of the bench, feeling tired of the whole affair and wondering what sort of nuisance the execution of this will was going to be. I ought to have insisted on knowing the beneficiary. Supposing the old lady had after all been of disturbed mind, and had left it to a non-existent person? Or supposing she had been a practical joker and left all her estate to the Pope or the President of the United States or the government of Soviet Russia or somebody serving a life sentence in prison?

At the worst it could be exceedingly tiresome and at best I should look an awful fool.

I heard footsteps and looked up to see the ward sister approaching.

"She's dead," I said as I looked up at her face.

"Yes. It's a mercy, really. Doctor asked me to tell you and to say she'll be coming to see you in about five minutes' time if you'll be good enough to wait. She thought you would like to speak to her."

"I would indeed," I said. "Thank you."

The sister departed.

She's dead, I said to myself, shocked and shaken as if Miss Porlock had been an old and dear friend and not just a client of a few hours' standing. Then I scolded myself. You're a fool, Harry. You've got into an absurdly emotional and overwrought state. Take a grip on yourself or you'll be heading for a nervous breakdown.

I stood up to seek relief in movement. And then suddenly I sat down again. She's dead and you can open that envelope.

My fingers were shaking so much that I could hardly tear back the flap. I pulled the single folded sheet half out of the envelope and half-opened the fold so that I could read what was inside. The small scholarly handwriting was less firm than it was in the letter on our file, but it was legible enough, and underneath her insertion Miss Porlock had signed her full name and the two witnesses had added theirs.

Part of my mind was taking this in and noting that it was a perfectly valid legal document, while the rest of me was shaken all over again with shock and disbelief and very great distress.

I suppose I must have pushed the document back into the envelope and returned the envelope to my briefcase and shut the case, but I had no consciousness of having done any of these things, nor of doing anything at all between the moment when I read Miss Porlock's writing and the moment when I heard Dr. Watson's voice, full of concern.

"Mr. Johnson . . . Mr. Johnson, are you ill?"

"I'm awfully sorry, but I'm afraid I am. I must have been ill for some time without realising it. Not physically, but—"

"Can you walk a little way? Just across the car park?"

I stood up and picked up my briefcase. That was

when I realised that I must have put Miss Porlock's will back without knowing I was doing it.

"I can walk all right," I said. "I just seem to have . . . lost myself. I feel like a zombie. I'm awfully sorry."

She took me by the arm. We passed through two lots of swing doors and then into the open air. It felt fresh and damp and I began to revive a little.

"I'm being a nuisance to you," I said. "I mustn't take up any more of your time. Perhaps if I could sit somewhere quietly for a few minutes. . . . I've had a bit of a shock. I think I'll be fit to drive once I've got over it."

"You can sit in my flat and drink some very sweet weak tea, which is the classic remedy for shock. I'm going to have some too."

"But aren't you going off duty? I mean—"

"I'm on duty all night. On call, rather. If I'm needed they'll call me."

I didn't really want to argue. I knew I was not fit to go home yet. And what better place to have my long-delayed nervous collapse than in a hospital alongside one of the resident medical staff? In that respect, at least, Miss Miranda Porlock had done me a good service.

By the time we came into the doctor's living-room I was sufficiently recovered to take some notice of my surroundings. There were no photographs, no pictures or ornaments. Only a few shelves of books gave evidence of personal tastes. Students coming up to university leave greater marks of their individuality within half an hour of occupying their rooms than Dr. Grace Watson appeared to have left upon hers.

On another occasion I might have found it cold and unwelcoming, but in my present condition I found it extraordinarily soothing. This impersonal institutional room made no demands upon the eye or on the mind. Here one could rest as if in a vacuum, outside time and place. No need to comment on the owner's taste, no need to admire, to react in any way.

Dr. Watson came in with a tray and we drank the sweet tea and ate some plain biscuits, and she told me that Miranda Porlock had died almost immediately after I had left the ward.

"I'm glad," I said.

"Oh, so am I." Again that little flash of feeling in the grey eyes under the thick, greying auburn hair.

"It means a lot to you," I ventured, "that death should be quick and comparatively painless?"

"Yes."

"I feel strongly about it too, but then, I'm not a doctor."

She made no reply, and for a moment I wondered whether this rather thoughtless remark had perhaps given offence, since it might be taken as implying that doctors generally were lacking in compassion, but when I looked up at her I had the impression that she had not even heard me, but had withdrawn into her own thoughts. For several minutes neither of us spoke. It was a restful silence, not an awkward one. At last she said: "Does this sort of job often come your way?"

"It's not uncommon," I replied, "for people to delay making a will until it's almost too late, but I've never experienced anything quite so dramatic as this evening. Nor found myself so deeply affected by it."

"It triggered something off?"

"Very much so. But I don't know why."

"Do you want to try to find out? Do you want to tell me?"

This was said in an unemotional, matter-of-fact voice. There was a consulting-room atmosphere about the room. It was the sort of voice that I myself adopted and the sort of atmosphere that I tried to create when a client turned up in a nervous and distressed state of mind.

"Yes, I think I would like to tell you," I replied. "I'll try to stick to the essentials and make it short."

I thought for a moment before going on. Then I said: "I had a comfortable home and a good up-bringing and I went into the profession I wanted and married the girl I wanted and although there were various ups and downs my life was as contented and free from trouble as any human life can possibly be expected to be."

"But it isn't now?"

"No. That is until about a year ago. Just over a year ago."

The weakness came over me again and I had to stop talking for a little while in order to overcome it. Dr. Watson sat with her chin resting on her hand and stared at the carpet and said nothing.

"Thanks," I said. "I think I'll be all right now. I'll begin at that point, with the death of my wife."

CHAPTER 2

Imogen was murdered.

Actually it was recorded as an accidental death, because that's the way our legal system works, but I have never been able to think of it as anything but murder. If you direct a lethal weapon at someone because he or she happens to be in your way, and that weapon causes severe wounds, and you go on your way without making any attempt to prevent those wounds from becoming fatal, then, in my opinion, and this is my professional opinion as well as my personal opinion, you have committed the act of murder, because that is what the word means—killing—and it doesn't matter whether it was unintentional or unprovoked or whether you never even knew the victim at all.

Hold it, Harry. You are becoming obsessed. Of course the law has to take account of intentions and accidents and unsound minds and all the rest of it. This stupid, blunt weapon of law has to try to refine itself if human society is to be tolerable at all. Otherwise we are left with nature red in tooth and claw, with the blood feud, with every man free to take his own revenge. . . .

Keep cool, now. This nice, calm, sensible doctor has offered to listen to you, really listen to you, as no

one else has ever done because they have been so
frightened of it all, frightened of the fact that it
could so easily have happened to themselves, frightened of your grief and of your fury.

You must not tell her that Imogen was murdered.
You must tell her the truth as it is stated in the rec-
ords: Imogen was knocked down in the road by a
hit-and-run driver and left there to die.

It happened on Friday, the twenty-first of March,
at approximately half past three in the afternoon.
The approximate time was fixed by a number of expert witnesses, all heavily relying on the opinion of
the woman who found her. This woman happened to
be a district nurse, driving back from a visit to a patient. She did what she could for Imogen, but it was
too late. The internal bleeding had gone too far.

Our house is on the outskirts of Swanhurst, up a
steep and winding road. It happened about half a
mile further up the hill. Imogen was out walking the
dog, a little brown mongrel whom we called Mouse.
She took him up on the Downs most afternoons and
along this piece of road she always kept him on the
lead.

And she always kept to the grass verge herself.
The road was not dangerous for either drivers or
walkers, provided elementary precautions were
taken. We had lived for fifteen years in that house
and never known an accident in that place before.
But on that date and at roughly that time somebody
drove down that hill at an unwarranted speed and
came off the road onto the edge of the grass and
knocked Imogen over and ran over her, literally ran

over her, and then went on down the road and disappeared for ever.

It was a dry day, but there were certain traces of tyres to be seen, and the police reconstructed the accident and decided on the type of car; and they broadcast appeals for information and made all the enquiries they possibly could.

All to no avail. People tried to be helpful, but it all boiled down to nothing when investigated in detail. Imogen's murderer was never found and there was no witness to her killing.

No. That is not quite true. There was one witness. A dumb witness. The little brown mongrel dog lay whimpering with his head against her arm. He was injured too. The kind district nurse took him to the vet for me and when I called there next day they said he might have a chance to pull through but that he would never walk properly again.

I blame myself there. At first I simply could not bear to let Mouse go. I brought the dog back from the vet's, bandaged and drugged and with various pills that I was told to give him, and I arranged my whole existence around the search for Imogen's killer and the caring for Mouse.

The first was useless. The second was useless too, and I ought never to have dragged out the poor creature's sufferings. And yet in a way that little sick animal was my salvation, so I hope I may be forgiven.

He protected me against the friends who wanted me to leave my home and come and stay with them, and he gave me a purpose for coming home. Above all, he gave me the chance to behave as I needed to

behave—to talk and talk, not to myself, which I
could not have done because it would have frightened me too much to lose all control, but to talk to
the dog.

This is what animals do for us. We can talk to
them when we can never talk to ourselves or to other
human beings. And so I talked to Mouse, hour after
hour, gently, not loudly, stroking the rough coat.

"Can't you tell me? Oh, Mouse, do try to tell me!
It was your very own mistress, our very own dearest
—that's who it was, Mouse, and we've lost her—we've
got to go on alone, Mouse, you and me. But we'll
talk of her—we'll never stop thinking and talking of
her. . . ."

That was how I drooled over the dog, and this
nice Australian doctor, who sat and listened without
making any comment, was the first person I had ever
confessed it to.

On the fifth day, as arranged, I took the dog to the
vet. He examined him and talked of possible opera-
tions, but I could see from his face that he was longing for me to sign the consent form for the dog's
release. And so I said goodbye to Mouse and came
home and wept a little, as I had not been able to do
for Imogen, not until over a year had passed.

Poor little dog! Thank you, Mouse; you kept me
going. By the fifth day I had begun to grow a shell.
And yet perhaps it might have been better if. . . .

At this point I put a question to Dr. Watson.

"If I hadn't had the dog, would I have collapsed
at once and got it over with instead of hanging on
for a year and collapsing now?"

She thought for a moment before saying: "I don't

think one can look at it that way. I think one has to
be grateful for anything that helps at such a time. I
am glad you had the dog and I don't think you were
wrong to try to keep him alive a little while."

"Thank you," I said. "That comforts my mind. Es-
pecially coming from you."

I glanced up at her and I thought she coloured
slightly. For a moment I thought of explaining that I
was not trying to get into any personal relationship
but that I only meant I could tell from her treatment
of Miss Porlock that she did not believe in forcing
suffering creatures to go on breathing any longer
than was necessary, and therefore her approval was
worth having.

But this was a digression. Not now. Perhaps later,
if there was to be any later. Perhaps this acquaintance begun over a deathbed was going to develop
into a personal relationship after all. Or perhaps I
should go away from this strange confessional in this
clinical-looking room and find that with a clear conscience and a quiet mind I could bring my own life
to an end. But at the moment it did not matter
which road I took. I was launched on a task—the re-
creation of Imogen—and must not be deflected from
it.

Perhaps we had been too selfish in our happiness.
We had no children and never felt the lack. Mouse
was the last of a succession of well-loved pets. I met
Imogen at college, where we were both studying
law. She continued to practise for the first twenty-
five years of our married life and then, almost apolo-
getically, asked if I would mind very much if she
gave up and stayed at home to look after the garden

and be lazy. We had plenty of money and I could have retired too if I had wanted to, but I rather enjoyed the human contacts in my job, whereas she, with the better legal brain, had never quite overcome her shyness with strangers.

Her retirement changed nothing except that she had more time to practise her cello than I my violin. We were enthusiastic amateur musicians, and together with a similar couple who were our closest friends, played quartets every Sunday afternoon and evening.

Of course they wanted me to carry on with the music after Imogen died, and perhaps I really was being obstinate and self-pitying when I refused. But I felt as if I had no choice. My fingers simply refused to hold the bow. You can carry on with your profession with a deadened heart and mind, but you cannot go on doing the things you do for love. My relationship with this couple became strained and eventually dwindled to a rather uncomfortable evening together once a month.

Other friendships went the same way. People got tired of trying to help me and I don't blame them. I honestly think that the manner of her death was particularly hard to take. It left me with this terrible legacy of vengeful fury against an unknown person. Or persons.

The unknownness is intolerable. If cancer had been the enemy who took her I would have joined with others thus bereaved and worked towards its conquest. If she had lost her life in saving another's, I should have been proudly stricken. If it had been as it was but they had found the poor wretch who drove that car, then at least I should have known my enemy, and perhaps, knowing him, have been able, in the midst of all my feelings of revenge, to see him as a fellow human creature; and seeing him so, might have hoped that one day I would feel in myself the healingness of forgiving.

But I can see nothing and nobody. I never will be able to. There is nothing but blinded and paralysed revenge.

At this point I again fell silent for a while, and Dr. Watson spoke.

"It's a very terrible thing to have to come to terms with, but there are those who have to live with something that is perhaps even worse."

"You mean when their nearest and dearest has committed suicide?"

It was strange that I should know instantly what she meant.

"Yes," she replied. "If one could make a league table of griefs—and actually I don't think one can or ought to compare them, because to the sufferer all griefs are intolerable and comparison only makes them feel worse—but if one could make such a table, then I would think the suicide of someone very near would be the hardest of all to take."

"And supposing the would-be suicide has no one very close to him. Is he still committing an act of cruelty to others when he takes his own life?"

I wondered as I asked this if she was reading my thoughts: I wondered if she was talking with a purpose in mind.

"I didn't say he was committing an act of cruelty," she replied. "I think it shows great lack of imagination and great lack of compassion when people blame suicides for being selfish and inconsiderate towards others."

"Then, you don't think self-destruction is wrong?"

"I don't think it's a matter of right or wrong at all. It's a matter of the human mind and will driven beyond its endurance. You can't blame it any more than you can blame a piece of elastic for snapping when it is stretched beyond its strength."

I leaned forward in my armchair. It was a students' common-room type of chair, hard-wearing, moderately comfortable, less pretentious than that of a hotel lounge.

"Look, are you saying that there could be other circumstances, not only suicide, where people cannot be held responsible for their actions because the string has snapped? Murder under intense provocation, for example?"

She smiled faintly. "The law takes account of it, doesn't it?"

I remained tensely waiting, knowing she was going to say something more. The grey eyes were thoughtful. It was an interesting face, not a beautiful one. The skin was lined and weatherbeaten; the nose and mouth were out of symmetry and too large. But the mind behind it was coming to meet me in a way that no other mind had done since Imogen died. I was beginning to see some light.

Not hope. Just light. I felt on the verge of some sort of intellectual resolution, as if a problem was sorting itself out in my mind. That was all. I still could not see any hope of a future.

"Of course I believe that people can be provoked

beyond endurance into violent action that can lead to another's death," she said at last. "But I wouldn't like to have to decide on the breaking point. How on earth do you test human endurance? It's not like putting weights on strands of rope or elastic."

I relaxed back in my chair. She had not failed me. Ever since Imogen's death, well-meaning people had been telling me what I ought to think and feel and do, which really meant what they believed they would think or feel or do were they in my circumstances. None of them had ever said they didn't know, or countered one question by asking another.

"But in the case of your wife it wasn't a killing under intense provocation," went on Dr. Watson. "It's difficult to imagine any extenuating circumstances."

"I suppose the driver could have had some sort of fainting fit or blackout, from which he or she recovered quickly enough to go on driving, but without knowing that the car had killed somebody."

This theory had been put forward at the time and I had rejected it vehemently. I needed the unknown villain on whom to throw all my anger and my longing for revenge. It was the only thing that kept me going. But now, for the first time, I was calmly facing the possibility that there was no such villain. I had actually stated the case myself.

"What do you do when you can't blame anybody?" I added.

"I don't know. Blame yourself, I suppose. Or invent the Devil."

"I don't believe in Fate or the Devil, and I can't blame myself for Imogen's death."

"Of course you can't." She surveyed me for a moment or two. "Harry Johnson," she went on presently, "I do feel most truly sorry for you and I only wish I could help."

It felt like a dismissal but I made no movement. All was dead and dark within me again, but I could not bear to leave the place where I had seen that glimmer of light. Perhaps if we talked a little longer I might recapture it.

"You have helped me," I said. "Very much indeed and I'm deeply grateful."

Even as I spoke I could hear in my voice the chilling brightness of insincerity. This was the way I spoke to sympathetic friends who longed so much to be of use, for human contact one must have, even though a great glass wall separates one from all others. I wanted people to think they were helping me, for after all it was not their fault, and they needed to believe they were of use.

In my saner moments I understood this. We are impossible creatures, we the bereaved. Whatever people do, we take amiss. The would-be comforters simply cannot win. We resent it if they seem to be not sympathetic enough, and when they try so hard to sympathise we turn on them and say they cannot possibly understand. We make it so difficult for them and yet at the same time we need them. Oh, how we do need them!

Don't misunderstand me, my mind was crying out to Dr. Watson even while I heard the falseness in my own voice. Please bear with me. Please don't drift away. Please go on trying to help me.

She responded in her unique way to my unspoken plea.

"I don't think I've helped very much, but I do think there is some change taking place in you, possibly for the better. If so, then it is Miss Porlock whom you ought to be thanking, not me."

Miranda Porlock. I had very nearly forgotten her and her extraordinary last will and testament. Miranda Porlock was the reason why I was sitting opposite Dr. Grace Watson now.

My professional mind began to function again. Miss Porlock was dead and I was her executor. The thought of carrying out her wishes made me blench, but always supposing I didn't succumb to the suicidal impulse, it would be my job to implement the will. Meanwhile the less said about it the better, except that I would like to know whether the two witnesses had actually seen Miss Porlock's insertion in the space that I had left blank.

"I do indeed wish I could thank Miss Porlock," I said. "I wish I had known her. Had she been in hospital for long?"

"Only a week, and she would not have been here at all if she hadn't collapsed in the street—or, rather, in the public gardens behind the town hall—and someone passing by sent for an ambulance. She knew she was very ill but she wanted to die at home. Alone. Some people really do want it that way."

"I know. It's a pity she didn't get her wish."

But if Miranda Porlock had collapsed and died in her own house, and presumably intestate, then this evening's events would never have taken place. I would not have had this great problem that I had to face over the will, but on the other hand, I would not have experienced this thawing out, painful as it was, of my own deadness.

And above all, I would not have met Dr. Grace Watson.

On balance, for my own sake, I could not help but be glad that Miranda Porlock had collapsed in a public place and not alone at her home.

"It's time I went," I said, getting up from my chair. "Even if you're on call all night, you'll want to get some rest."

"You are living on your own?" She had stood up too and was looking at me rather anxiously.

"Yes, but I promise and swear—I swear you the most solemn of oaths, Grace Watson, that I am not going to make any suicidal attempt tonight. If I feel an overwhelming urge to go and jump off Beachy Head, then I will telephone you. Does that satisfy you?"

"I suppose it will have to."

We moved towards the door. "That was a strange business over the will," she went on thoughtfully. "Do you anticipate having trouble with it?"

"It's too early to say." To be noncommittal seemed the best policy. It rather looked as if she had not seen the name of the beneficiary and I didn't want to tell an outright lie. "But it's always possible that I shall have to call on you and Sister Jenkins as witnesses to the signature," I added. "Particularly as witnesses to the signature to the insertion that she insisted on making herself. Extraordinary business. Most unorthodox. At the moment, I can't think of any precedent. Did you see what she wrote, by the way?"

Grace Watson shook her head. "Neither did Sister Jenkins. I'm bound to admit that we were both bursting with curiosity. Although even if we had seen it, I suppose it would have meant nothing to us."

"What actually happened when my back was turned?" I asked.

"You saw how we were holding Miss Porlock up and leaning over the bedtable so that she could write?"

"Yes, that's the last I saw."

"Well, I was holding the paper steady for her, and she suddenly got an access of strength and pushed my hand away quite vigorously and held her left hand over the paper, and leant even further forward and wrote under the shelter of her left hand. It was a great effort for her, but she was determined to do it. When she'd finished, she held her left hand over the words she had just written and gave the pen to me and I signed my name and then Sister Jenkins signed hers."

"But Miss Porlock had signed first?"

"Oh yes. We could see her signature as we signed, but nothing else. Then she turned the paper down so that only the last line was visible, in your handwriting, and we repeated the process at the end of the document. Was that all right?"

"Perfectly. You don't need to witness the document, only the signature to the document. In fact she didn't really need a solicitor at all. She could quite well have done the whole thing without me.

Anybody can make a will, on any piece of paper, and expressed in any terms, providing it's signed and the signature witnessed."

"And providing the witnesses are not beneficiaries," she said with a smile.

"Very true, but I doubt if Miss Porlock would have made that elementary mistake. She seems to have known exactly what she was doing."

We had reached the entrance to the building. It was raining again, and the grey surface of the car park shone in the light from the hospital windows.

"Oh, by the way," I said, "did Miss Porlock have any relatives?"

"Nobody has been to visit her or has enquired after her," was the reply, "but she was asked for the name of her next of kin as soon as she was fit to speak. I can't recall it at the moment, but I could find out and let you know. Would tomorrow morning do?"

"Tomorrow would do fine."

"Good night, then, Harry Johnson, and take care."

"Good night, Grace Watson, and thank you."

She gave a slight shrug and disappeared into the building. I hurried through the rain to where I had left the car, got in, and drove home slowly, taking particular care with the awkward, uphill turn into the drive. I felt weak and rather dazed, as if I had just wakened from a long, drugged sleep and was not yet fully myself. When I had shut the garage and was hurrying along the wet gravel path to the front door, I suddenly turned my steps towards the front gate instead.

The rain was coming faster and my briefcase was

heavy, but my impulse to revisit the spot was over-whelming. Ten minutes' walk up the steep, winding road. It was dark now and there were no street lamps and I had no torch, but I knew every stone of the way. Again and again I had gone there, unable to stop myself, but knowing it would only make me worse. I had stood on the grass by the side of the road and pictured the crash and poured fresh fuel upon the hatred burning in my heart.

After that I had come home exhausted and had sat for a long time doing nothing, thinking nothing, star-ing at nothing.

Tonight it was different. I reached the place and stood a few moments, panting because I had hurried up the hill. The presence of Imogen was all around me, but I did not picture her death. In fact I scarcely thought at all. I just stood there, weak and passive.

After a while I became conscious that I was very wet, and I moved slowly down the hill, driven by the primitive need for shelter. It was while I was in this non-thinking, almost dreamlike state that the voice came to me: a clear, firm voice that sounded as if it were somebody speaking in my ear.

"You are going to find out what happened," it said, "and that will set you free."

So certain was I that the words had come from outside myself that I stopped and peered around in the darkness of the lane. When I was satisfied that there was nobody there, I walked briskly home, said good night to my neighbour who was just driving in at his gate, and came into my house with no other feeling than relief at being out of the rain. The chill of its emptiness had left me at last. I changed into dry clothes, fried some sausages and heated up a packet of mashed potatoes, and ate this uninspiring meal with a good appetite. Then I made coffee and poured out some liqueur, lit a cigarette, and lit the gas fire in the living-room, and sat down to listen to a Haydn quartet. It was one that we had used to play together.

"That's the bit where Imogen always had trouble," I said to myself at the beginning of the last movement.

It was painful, but not excruciatingly so. When the music had come to an end, I switched off the record player, opened my briefcase, and took out the envelope containing Miranda Porlock's will. Very deliberately I refilled my glass before I opened the fold of the paper. Then I laid it on my knee and read in my own handwriting:

". . . give and bequeath my house and all its contents and all my real and personal estate and everything of which I die possessed to . . ."

Then in Miss Porlock's handwriting:

". . . Harry Johnson, of 4 St. Martin's Terrace, Swanhurst in the County of Sussex. . . ."

I shook my head, took another sip from my glass, and began to laugh to myself. It was not hysterical laughter, but it was not quite under my control and I was glad when it stopped. I replaced the document, turned off the fire, and went upstairs to bed.

"It's going to be awkward, to say the least of it, Imogen," I said, "if there turns out to be some hopeful next of kin. I wonder what tomorrow will bring forth?"

This was the first time since Imogen's death that I had talked to her aloud in this way. It felt quite right and natural and it didn't upset me at all. I went to sleep with my mind full of the strange woman who had come so briefly into my life, and I slept soundly for a long time.

It was the first time since Imogen's death that I had gone to sleep with the feeling that I really wanted to find out what was going to happen tomorrow. If this means that I am cured, was my last waking thought, then it is curiosity that is the great healer, not time.

CHAPTER 3

At ten o'clock the following morning, Jenny rang through to my office to tell me that there was a Dr. Watson on the line. I had been expecting the call and was conscious of a quickening of anticipation as I waited for it to be put through. But when I heard the voice I was conscious of slight disappointment. She sounded friendly but formal.

"Mr. Johnson? I promised you some information. The name is Mervyn Porlock, a nephew, of an address in London, and I believe he will be calling on you in person shortly."

"You've been in touch with him?"

No doubt my voice sounded equally formal, and I could not help wondering whether she, too, was slightly disappointed. This is idiotic, I told myself: I know nothing whatever about Dr. Watson, far far less than she knows about me. Widowed, divorced, unmarried, or with a husband and family in Australia? Her personal circumstances might be anything. I didn't even know whether she was on a long-term appointment as a resident medical officer at the Queen Mary Hospital or whether she was simply standing in for somebody and would be clearing off at any minute.

This last thought frightened me, and I had to remind myself that she was a responsible person, and that in any case we were bound together in a professional relationship in connection with Miss Porlock's will. Grace Watson would be a vital witness in any possible court case; she knew that, and she would not just go out of my life without leaving an address.

She told me that they had tried last night to get in touch with Mr. Porlock but without success. It was not until an hour and a half ago that they had spoken to him at last, and his first question had been, "Did my aunt leave a will?"

"Very natural in the circumstances," I said cautiously. "Did you explain to him?"

"No. I said I could not enter into discussions about the legal affairs of deceased patients but that I knew his aunt had a solicitor, and I gave him your name and address. I hope I did right?"

"Perfectly. Thank you very much. Are you expecting him at the hospital?"

"He didn't say he was coming," she replied, "and I was wondering whether you would like me to hand over her possessions to you, as her executor. There's not very much. Just the clothes she was wearing when she was brought in and her handbag with a few odds and ends, including a bunch of keys."

Keys! How on earth could I have been so remiss as not to think of the keys to the house I had inherited from Miss Porlock! All these years of law practice, all my experience of the deviousness of human nature, particularly of human nature disappointed in its expectations, and yet it had never entered my mind last night to ask for Miss Porlock's possessions. But then, I had been in a very strange state of mind all yesterday evening. And fortunately no harm was done, thanks to Grace Watson.

"Yes, I think I'd better have her things," I said as calmly as I could. "I'll come and collect them straight away, and when Mr. Porlock turns up, then I can hand them over to him if he wants them."

This last was for the benefit of whoever might be listening on the line. In fact I had no intention of handing over anything whatever to Miss Porlock's nephew. We arranged that I should call at the hospital reception desk, and Grace hoped to be free to come and see me herself. The formal note had left her voice and I had the pleasing feeling that we were somehow in league together. When I put the telephone down, I found myself in a state of eagerness and interest in life such as I had never expected to experience again.

It is sad, but true, that one's state of mind tends to attract the sort of happenings suited to itself. Be fearful, and you will meet with reactions that justify your fear; suspicious, and people will shun you and make you even more so. Feel in yourself a lively interest in what is going on around, and you will find everybody rushing to tell you their affairs.

That was what happened to me after my telephone conversation with Dr. Watson. Geoff came in for a little gossip about our clients, and I was just about to ask him to give me some more information about Miss Porlock when my secretary, Marilyn, turned up with a long string of queries and stayed to chat as well. Geoff then remembered an appointment, but one of the junior clerks arrived and took his place. It was turning into a sort of house-warm-ing party. Word had gone round that Harry Johnson was himself again.

I didn't want any of them to know I was going out to see a lady doctor. They'd have had me married off in no time. In the end I just got up and said: "Marilyn, I'm late for an appointment. If a Mr. Porlock turns up, hang on to him. I shan't be long."

Not that he's likely to need any persuasion to remain, I thought as I drove quickly to the hospital: Mr. Mervyn Porlock must be a very worried man.

At the reception desk I saw the back of a white coat, and above it was dark auburn hair with grey streaks in it.

Grace turned round and smiled at me. "You're feeling better. I can see you are."

"I'm miles better. Just sorry I went and had a nervous breakdown on you last night. I don't think it's going to happen again."

"I don't think so either, but even if it does, it doesn't matter. Have you time for coffee?"

"Not really," I said, "and I'm sure you haven't either. But let's go and have some."

We walked across the car park, laughing a little and telling each other that we felt as if we were playing truant. The sun had broken through the clouds and it looked like being a glistening spring day, but I no longer had the sense of dread of the bright summer days to come. It is when all is blackness within that the outside light cannot be endured. Of all the joys and blessings of creation, I do not think there is one to compare with the moment when one knows, with absolute certainty, that the

day will come when once again one will enjoy the
sun.

I did not say this to my companion, but I had the
feeling that, had I done so, she would have known
what I meant.

"Only coffee powder," she said. "It's quicker."

I took the cup and sat on the arm of a chair.

"And here's Miss Porlock's things," she went on.
"The clothes are in this parcel, but I thought you'd
like the handbag separately."

"I would indeed. Thanks."

It was a dark brown leather bag that had once
been good but was much worn. I opened it, noted
the key-ring and several other items, and closed it
again.

"What did you make of Miss Porlock's nephew?" I
asked.

"He sounded as greedy and impatient as expec-
tant relatives usually are. Perhaps I shouldn't be too
unkind about him, just because it is such a commonplace. You really are better this morning, Harry. I
was quite worried about you last night."

"So was I at first. And then a strange thing happened."

I told her quickly about my impulse to visit the
place where Imogen died, and about the resolution
that seemed to come from right outside myself but
that was now strong within me and strengthening
every hour.

"It sounds like a good, healthy reaction," she said
rather guardedly. "As long as you don't raise your
hopes too high."

"You mean, why should I think I can find out the

truth now, so long after it happened, and when all the official enquiries have failed?"

"Well, it does sound a little optimistic."

"It sounds quite crazy," I exclaimed, "but there are two things that make me feel it's not entirely impossible. First of all, I'm in the right state of mind. It's truth I want now, not revenge, and I think truth is easier to seek than vengeance, because one can be more whole-hearted about it and one isn't hampered by feelings of guilt. And the second thing is that I've got a hunch. Don't you find sometimes in your job that you have an instinct about something—sometimes apparently against all reason?"

"Yes, I get these feelings. Mostly they turn out to be wrong, but occasionally they are justified."

"If I'm wrong there'll be no harm done," I said. "I'm not going to stand up in court and cry, '*J'accuse!*' If I'm right—well, we'll have to wait and see. But the feeling is very strong and I'm going to follow it up."

"Then, I can only wish you luck," she said quietly.

"May I tell you how I get on with Mr. Mervyn Porlock?"

She smiled. "I must confess I'm very curious."

"Do you ever have any free time? There's rather a nice fish dish I could make if you'd come and have dinner with me. Or would you prefer a restaurant?"

"I'd like your fish dish, and I'm free tomorrow evening."

"That's fine. I promise not to weep all over you again. It's your turn now. If you want to take it, that is," I added hastily as I saw her expression change and a shut-in look replace its natural openness.

I thought about that look as I drove back to the office and came to the conclusion that there was some hurt in her life that she did not want to reveal. If that was the case, then she was safe from me. There were plenty of other things to talk about apart from our own personal problems.

When I reached St. Martin's Terrace, I found that my usual parking place was now filled. This centrally situated row of Victorian houses was almost entirely occupied by offices, and of course everybody drove to work in Swanhurst, even if they lived only a few blocks away. Those of us who worked in the Terrace became absurdly indignant if we could not find a space to put our cars, and when the local council threatened us with a total ban on parking, our anger and apprehension knew no bounds. Great disasters could be endured, but the removal of our parking spaces was felt to be intolerable.

I did not recognise the white estate car that was standing on what I regarded as my own territory, but of course I took an instant dislike to its owner. In a nearby side street, all of one and a half minutes' walk from the office, I left my Renault with the parcel of Miss Porlock's clothing locked in the boot. The contents of the handbag, I had transferred to my jacket pockets.

There were the keys—half a dozen of them in a leather holder; a purse with very little money in it; a wallet containing a cheque-book and a few photographs; a small memo pad; a ball-point pen; and a few visiting cards, dog-eared and yellow with age.

No make-up of any sort, not even a pocket mirror. No handkerchief. Further clues as to the life and

character of this woman who had made me her heir
would have to wait until I had a chance to inspect
the real estate portion of my inheritance: Beth's Cottage, in the village of Mill Green, five miles from
Swanhurst.

As soon as I could get away from the office, I intended to go there. Meanwhile there was Mr. Mervyn Porlock to be faced.

Of course the white Ford estate car was his. Marilyn, who had been in my room watching my abortive
arrival from the window, told me that.

"He's in the waiting-room," she added. "He
wouldn't believe Jenny when she said you were out
and he very nearly didn't believe me." She made a
face of disgust. Marilyn is nineteen years old and,
like Brenda, a bit cocksure and officious, but she has
good judgement about people.

"What's he like?" I asked.

She made a face again.

"I quite appreciate that you don't like him," I
said, "but could you try to overcome your feelings
and expand a little?"

She likes me to talk like this—mock pompously—so
that she can enjoy herself mimicking me.

"He's like this," she said, tilting her head up and
looking down her nose at me. "Thinks he's God's gift
to women. I think he's a male chauvinist pig."

"Can an m.c.p. be attractive to women?" I asked.

"I didn't say he was attractive," she replied. "I
said he fancies he is."

"But presumably he must have some basis for his
supposition. Is he good-looking?"

"Yuk," said Marilyn, lowering her nose.

I began to laugh. It seemed a long time since Marilyn and I had had such a light-hearted and friendly chat and I was very tempted to keep Miss Porlock's nephew waiting while we continued it. But conscience—and curiosity—had to be satisfied.

"Do you think you can overcome your abhorrence of this gentleman sufficiently to go and inform him that Mr. Johnson will see him now," I said, "or shall I ask Jenny to send him in?"

"I'll tell him," she cried, allowing her features to revert to their normal, pleasant shape and dancing out of the room like the child she still was.

She's happy, I thought; I believe she really does like working for me and she can see I am feeling better.

"Good morning," I said a moment later, getting up from my chair and smiling and holding out my hand. "I'm sorry you've been kept waiting—though I must also say that you are lucky I am able to see you at all without an appointment. It is not usual."

My hand was ignored and my words received a sort of grunt of acknowledgement. Enemies at first sight. Or even before first sight. Could Mr. Mervyn Porlock possibly have known what his aunt intended to do with her money?

I indicated the chair at the other side of my desk and he sat down on it, sitting sideways to the desk, and thus giving me the benefit of his profile.

It was a most impressive one. The hair was very dark and had been treated to an expert cutting and setting, and he wore a grey suit that had been similarly dealt with. He had clearly modelled himself on a well-known television personality.

He produced a small piece of pasteboard and flipped it across the desk at me. It read: "Mervyn Porlock. Consultant. Antiques and Objets d'Art. London, Paris, New York." Addresses were given for each of these cities.

"Thank you," I said, tucking the card into a corner of my blotter.

The profile turned slightly towards me and spoke. "I gathered from the hospital that my aunt had consulted you."

"That's right." With an effort I had stopped myself from saying: "Harry Johnson, Consultant. Small Town Solicitor. Elderly Clients and Human Curiosities." It would be a pleasure to give offence, but it would not be very sensible. After all, I held all the trump cards and he had nothing that I wanted. Except that I had this hunch that something in connection with Miranda Porlock's death was going to lead me to the truth about Imogen's death, and this man was Miranda Porlock's nearest living relative.

"It is some time since I had seen my aunt," he went on. "My business keeps me abroad a great deal."

The voice was rather like that of the television personality too. A not unpleasant voice, and it seemed now to be making some attempt to sound agreeable.

"I would imagine it does," I replied, "though I'm afraid I know nothing about the cosmopolitan world of antiques and art collecting."

If Marilyn had seen me, she would have accused me of overacting the part of small-town lawyer, but it seemed to be the best line to take.

"Well, I mustn't waste your time, Mr. Johnson,"
he said. "I'm sure time is a very precious commodity
for both of us. It will be obvious to you that I am interested in whether my aunt made a will. As far as I
know, she had made no will the last time I saw her,
which was about six months ago."

"She has consulted me since then," I said. "She
has made her will and I am named as executor. Her
only executor. She names no other. Neither does she
name any of her own kindred in the document.
Strictly speaking, I ought not to be telling you this at
this stage, but you are naturally very anxious to
know, and there is no reason why you should have a
wasted journey to Swanhurst. I am afraid I cannot
divulge any other of the contents of the document."

Stage solicitor stuff, I thought, wishing that Marilyn could be there to hear me. Mr. Porlock presented
me with his profile again. It showed no visible sign
of annoyance or disappointment, but there was no
further attempt at good humour, and when he spoke
I guessed that it was the same tone of voice that had
so offended Marilyn and Jenny.

"I suppose she's left all her money to a cats'
home," he said.

This remark annoyed me far more than anything
else he had said, probably because I remembered
making the same stupid joke, so-called, only the previous evening, and I was therefore feeling annoyed
with myself as well. Why is it always assumed that
rich and lonely old women should leave their money
to a cats' home? And what's the matter with cats,
anyway? Beautiful and useful creatures, very little
trouble to anybody, which is more than can be said

of an awful lot of human beings. And, in any case, you don't have "cats' homes." Not just like that. It would have to be a boarding kennel and cattery, or one of the various animal charities. . . .

With an effort I cut off my infuriated train of thought and repeated, politely I hoped: "I'm sorry. I'm afraid it is out of my power to tell you at this moment."

"Are you just being a cautious lawyer, Mr.—er— Jackson—I beg your pardon, Mr. Johnson, or do I detect a certain doubt about the contents of my aunt's will? Perhaps you are anticipating that it might be contested?"

I was slightly taken aback, not by the suggestion that the will might be contested, which was quite on the cards, but by the fact that he should say this to me now, for I had not expected open warfare to be declared quite so soon.

"I am sorry to have given you a false impression," I replied. "As far as I can tell at this stage, the matter is perfectly straightforward."

"Mr. Jackson—I beg your pardon, Mr. Johnson— am I not right in thinking that the contents of a will are public property, printed in the newspapers in fact, and that you cannot indefinitely persist in withholding this information from me?"

"Mr. Porlock, you are perfectly right in thinking that once probate has been granted, the contents of a will are open for everybody to see, but in the circumstances I do truly think it would be advisable for us to communicate through your solicitor rather than in person."

"Why? To make more work for the damned lawyers?"

I said nothing.

There was silence for a moment and then he added, more quietly but no less offensively: "Poor Aunt Miranda. She has been growing more and more forgetful and confused recently . . . it wouldn't be so difficult to persuade her . . . some people are unscrupulous enough. . . . So where and when did she actually make this will?" he concluded suddenly.

I had actually been expecting this question before now. Had he asked it earlier I might have prevaricated, but by this time I was sick of the interview and all I wanted was to get rid of him as soon as possible so that I could drive out to Mill Green and have a look round Beth's Cottage myself.

"Yesterday evening," I said. After all, he was bound to find out sooner or later.

"Yesterday evening."

I had succeeded in startling him into turning his full face towards me. It was much less worth looking at than the profile. The eyes were too close together and the mouth was peevish.

"But she only died yesterday evening," he went on. And then, a moment later: "That explains everything. I suspected as much." He stood up. "I shall follow your suggestion. You will be hearing from my solicitors."

And he left the room and the building without another word. Marilyn burst in just as I was picking up the telephone to contact her.

"Didn't I say—" she began rather breathlessly.

"Yes, you did, and I'm sure the opinion you

formed of him is correct, but I can't stay to talk now.
I've got to go urgently. In connection with the same
matter. Look, would you get hold of these people—
and these. . . ."

I quickly disposed of the next few hours' work.
Still scribbling in her notebook, Marilyn followed me
to the front door.

"But suppose we need to get hold of you. Can you
leave me a phone number?"

"I'll ring you back with it in half an hour," I said,
looking, from habit, for my car in the place where
the white Ford had been parked and cursing aloud
when I remembered that I had to go right round the
corner into the next road.

I had not seen in which direction Miss Porlock's
nephew had driven, but it seemed to me unlikely
that he would be going straight back to London.
There were two possible alternatives: Either he had
gone direct to the hospital to investigate the events
of last night in person, hoping, perhaps, to bully or
bribe some of the hospital staff into making state-
ments that could be helpful to him. Or he might
have gone straight to Miss Porlock's house. I could
well imagine that he would like to get there before I
did, but unless he was prepared to break in, he
would need to have a key, and I thought it unlikely
that she had given him one, since there did not appear to have been a close and trusting relationship
between them, in spite of his attempts to suggest
that they had been on good terms.

The quickest route to Mill Green led past my own
house, up the lane on which Imogen had died. I
didn't exactly suspect—or perhaps I did suspect, be-

cause the worst part about not knowing had been that I suspected everybody, even my old friends and colleagues—that Mervyn Porlock had been the driver of the car that killed her, but I did have a very strong feeling—the hunch that I had mentioned to Grace Watson—that Miranda Porlock had made me her heir for some very good reason: that her behaviour the previous evening was not simply some weird whim of a dying woman or even some last-minute decision of a lonely and friendless woman to leave her money to some "responsible" person, rather than let her nephew inherit, as he would have done if she had died intestate.

No. I believed that Miss Porlock had not only been legally capable and of sound mind. I believed that she had been strongly motivated. She wanted me, Harry Johnson, as a private citizen, not simply as a lawyer, to benefit in the only way that lay in her power to benefit anybody. How long she had been intending this I could not guess. Perhaps when I had had a chance to talk to Geoff about his interview with her last year I might have some clue. Or perhaps her decision was only recent; perhaps she had still been debating with herself whether or not to take this action when the collapse that had resulted in her being brought to hospital suddenly made it very urgent.

For most of the week that she had lain in hospital she had been too weak to do anything at all, too weak even to convey her wishes to anybody. So Grace had told me. That she had rallied enough to do so, on her dying day, was a tribute both to her own strength of purpose and to medical skill and nursing care.

At the very last moment, this strange old woman had made her will. Was it too fanciful to think that the beatific expression that had come over the dying woman's face had in fact been the reflection of a mind that had found its peace because it felt that a wrong had been righted?

Well, of course you can't say a wrong has been righted when the wrong consists of the loss of a beloved wife and the righting consists of the acquisition of a house and its contents and a certain portfolio of investments. Trying to fix monetary damages for human loss and suffering is rather like trying to please your God by offering sacrifices, or like trying to buy yourself love. The two things are on parallel lines. However, if one wants desperately to make amends and can see no other way. . . .

I was not going to drop my hunch. It had become my guiding light. The miracle was that I could follow it calmly, without the madness of revenge. That was Grace Watson's doing. It needed a stranger, somebody who had never known me and Imogen together, to take the wide and balanced view and guide me out of the quicksand.

Or perhaps it would have worked itself out in any case. Perhaps I was simply not of the stuff of which avengers are made. I could not stand Mervyn Porlock, but that was because of himself and not because of any harm he might have done me, or might still do me. And I rather liked Miranda Porlock in spite of the fact that she had caused me embarrassment, to say the least, by leaving me her estate both as heir and as executor.

Even if it should turn out that Miranda herself had been the one who caused Imogen's death, I believed I would still have a soft spot for her. There had been no driving licence in her handbag, but this did not mean she was not, or never had been, a car driver. Where had she been on the day in question? Where had Mervyn been? All these, and many other facts too, I was determined to find out.

It sounded a formidable task, but in many ways it was a more hopeful one than that which the police were faced with after the accident. They had vehicles to deal with; I had human beings. You can't learn much about a vehicle except its make and colour and condition and registration number and a few other such details. If these can't be juggled about to make a solution to the problem, then there is nothing more you can do.

Cars don't live and grow and change their minds, but human beings do. Cars, above all, do not feel guilty and try to make amends, but most human beings find it difficult to live with another's death on their consciences, and guilt takes many forms.

In the infinite possibilities contained within every human creature lay my own hope of discovering the truth.

CHAPTER 4

I had driven through Mill Green on a number of occasions, but I had never stopped there. I knew it only as a tiny village consisting of a church, an inn, a shop with a post office, a few houses grouped around a triangle of grass, and a few more houses scattered further afield. It had always seemed to me an exceptionally sleepy little place, and I could not remember ever having seen a human being there. But presumably there would be somebody in the inn or in the shop who could tell me where Beth's Cottage was.

In the event, I had no need to ask, nor even to go right into the village. I was driving slowly along the country lane, with farmland to my right and a wooded slope to my left, when I suddenly came across the house. The name was on a small wooden gate, on either side of which were high beech hedges. I pulled off the road onto the patch of grass outside the hedge and saw with relief that there was no white Ford estate car within sight. This did not necessarily mean that Mervyn was not somewhere in the neighbourhood or on his way, but at least I should have a chance to enter the house on my own.

There was no driveway, no sign of a garage. This pleased me too, since it diminished the likelihood that Miranda herself had been the driver I was seeking. Beth's Cottage stood alone, a mile or more from the village, and almost hidden from the road by the high hedge and the surrounding woods. I pushed open the little gate and caught my breath with delight.

The front garden was a mass of daffodils. They lit up the square grey flint house and gave it an air of light and life and welcome. Then I thought of the dying old woman and felt a stinging in the eyes. Don't try to resist these bouts of emotion, I said to myself; they are a sign of returning health of mind.

In the little gabled porch, I stood for a moment mentally wallowing in the pathos and futility of human lives and in the ever-recurring wonder of daffodils. At the same time, the active part of me was noting that there were no newspapers or milk bottles collected on the doorstep. Miss Porlock had collapsed in the public gardens in Swanhurst. She had presumably been intending to return home that day, so she would not have cancelled all services. Evidently she fetched whatever she needed for herself, but she could not stop Her Majesty's Mail delivering items to the house, and when I had opened the door, which was secured only with a Yale lock, I picked up several envelopes from the mat inside.

Then I looked quickly into the two main rooms on the ground floor: a living-room running from front to back of the house, and a smaller sitting-room opposite. The staircase, a single flight, led up to two bedrooms and a bathroom. First impressions can never be recaptured, but they can be very important for one's understanding of a person or of a situation. My first impression of Beth's Cottage was totally unex-

pected. I quite simply fell in love with the place.
From the back windows, there were views of more
daffodils, a neglected orchard, and beech woods beyond, just beginning to show a shimmer of green.
Chaffinches and sparrows perched hopefully on an
empty bird-table. They've missed their meals this
last week, I thought, and decided to see what I
could find for them in the kitchen.

It was as if I already felt the place to be my home.
It could indeed be my home if I wanted it: The
house was mine by law, or rather, it would be mine
when I had proved the will.

I don't know why I liked Beth's Cottage so much,
any more than I know why I liked Dr. Grace Watson's lined and irregular and life-worn face. Perhaps
it was because they happened to come into my vision at just the right moment, when the ice of bereavement was thawing at last and I could see with
eyes willing to see and to respond.

Miranda Porlock's house bore the imprint of herself. The furniture was a jumble of old and modern
and it had plainly been arranged for the convenience
of one increasingly feeble and sick old lady, and not
for showing off to visitors. I liked this, and I particularly liked the back bedroom, where she must have
been sleeping. The bed was placed just where I
would have put it myself—with a view out the window—and there was a sizeable table either side of it,
containing lamp and radio and Teasmade and bis-
cuit tins, and lots of books and writing-paper and
pens. There was also a used tumbler and a half-
empty whisky bottle and a jug of water with a thin
film of dust on the surface.

Among the books were several new mystery stories and some standard works of poetry, psychology, and philosophy. One of the last-named lay open at a discussion about natural justice, and several of the sentences had been heavily underlined. One of these sentences ran: "What, then, is this natural or ideal law to which man-made laws ought to strive to conform?" What indeed! And what had been the opinion of the woman who had lain in this bed? There was no television set. Miranda had evidently preferred to lie and read and think. No wonder people had considered her eccentric if not outright mad!

But she could not have been entirely without sentiment, because there were a few framed photographs on top of a dark oak linen chest just inside the door. Two of them were enlarged snapshots that looked like family groups, and I recognised the same faces as those in the snapshots in the handbag. The other one had not been stood up. In fact it still lay half covered by brown paper, as if she had been interrupted while opening the parcel that contained it. I pushed aside the wrappings and saw a much more pretentious affair than the family snapshots. It was a studio portrait in a narrow gold frame, and on it was written: "To M. with love from M."

That profile again. I turned over the wrapping and glanced at the date on the postmark. It was a little over a week earlier, shortly before Miranda had been taken to hospital.

Mervyn presenting his aunt with an expensive portrait of himself. Just the sort of thing he would do, but it didn't make me any the wiser. It might have been sent as a peace offering, an attempt to placate her. If I could only know how she herself felt about receiving the gift, that really would be of use. Or if I could only find some personal letters.

I went downstairs again, fully intending to have a closer look at the desk in the living-room, where it appeared that Miss Porlock kept some personal papers, but as I glanced at the open kitchen door I remembered those hungry birds, and my steps turned automatically towards the back of the house. The wild garden was pulling at me. I was longing to walk in it.

The kitchen was well equipped and contained several chairs. Comfort for an old lady, I thought. I opened a store cupboard and found a bag of peanuts. These would do. The finches could peck at them through the netting.

As I walked across the grass towards the nearest of the old apple trees, I had the impression of movement among the mass of shrubs that grew along the garden fence to my left. Rabbits? A fox? There must be plenty of wildlife around here, with the woods so near, and with a garden so secluded and so little occupied.

The apple tree was a very ancient one and looked as if it had never been pruned. Some of the branches drooped low over the ground, and the first bit of wood I touched cracked off in my hand. I stared up at the gnarled and peeling boughs and thought: Whole tree is crumbling—I'll have to be careful where I fix my hammock; for in my mind I was already lying in a hammock in the orchard, listening to the hum of bees on hot summer days.

I was roused from this foolish and untimely

dreaming by the distant sound of a telephone bell, and I suddenly remembered that I had promised to ring Marilyn at the office to let her know where I was. I half turned and had begun to duck my head to avoid a low-hanging branch when I felt a blinding pain at the side of my head. I could feel myself crumpling up and could even feel myself dropping the bag of nuts on the grass.

I also knew, before I lost consciousness, that I had not hit my head on the low bough but that something had hit me, and it connected in my darkening mind with the movement I believed I had seen in the bushes. My last thought before the blackness was of Miss Porlock's will, now locked in the office safe together with the contents of her handbag.

It was lucky for me that Marilyn was a bright girl who liked to take over the action herself.

She had guessed where I had gone, had found Miss Porlock's phone number from the file, and when she had received no reply to several calls, she had decided to use her lunch-hour to come and investigate, borrowing Jenny's mini for the purpose and driving the five miles much too quickly.

I can't have been actually unconscious for very many minutes, but I must have been lying on the grass too dizzy and dazed to move for the best part of half an hour. Marilyn actually found me staggering round the side of the house. The kitchen door had blown shut—or had somebody shut it?—but, rather to my surprise, the keys in their leather holder were still in my jacket pocket.

Marilyn gave a little squeal and ran towards me.

"You're bleeding," she said accusingly. "We'd better go straight to hospital."

"No, no. No need. I'll be all right in a little while."

I fished the keys out of my pocket and she helped me into the house and into a chair in the living-room and fetched water to bathe my head and found some antiseptic ointment to put on the wound.

"Honestly, Mr. Johnson," she said, "one can't let you out of one's sight for a moment. What on earth did you do?"

I debated whether to tell her my suspicions and decided against it. "Banged my head against the branch of an apple tree," I said. "Sounds daft, doesn't it?"

"It sounds too daft to be true." She considered me for a moment or two, her head on one side like a sparrow. Then she got up and walked to the far end of the long room and looked out into the back garden. "Can I get out?" she called out.

"Through the kitchen," I replied.

While she was gone, I shut my eyes and rested. I didn't think I was seriously hurt, but I felt very sorry for myself. It's a bit hard, I thought, that an old man can't begin to get over the death of his wife and have a little day-dream about the future without getting a clout on the head. Now, Harry, said the active part of my brain, which was beginning to function again, you know perfectly well that you were deliberately needling Mervyn Porlock in the hope that he might take some action that could give you a clue, and you ought to be pleased, because it looks as if he has done just that.

The white car, I thought, must have been hidden

along one of those woodland tracks, and he must
have been waiting behind the bushes in the garden.
Why not wait for me in the house? Because he had
no key and needed me to let him in. No burglary if it
could be avoided. And no assault that could be
proved against him. Very good at disappearing from
the scene of action without trace, was Mr. Mervyn
Porlock.

And yet there was something about the theory
that didn't quite fit in. Didn't fit in with my notion
that Miranda or Mervyn or somebody connected
with them had been responsible for Imogen's death,
I mean. The facts fitted, but the tone was somehow
wrong.

I played it all over in my mind. Mervyn badly
wanted to get into his aunt's house, as soon as he
knew of her death. He tried legitimate means first,
approaching her solicitor, presumably hoping to be
told that he was her heir. These means had failed,
and he had resorted to less acceptable methods.
Why did he want to get into the house? Because it
contained something he badly wanted, something
that he didn't want anybody else to know was there.

Obviously the house was full of things that he
would like to have—pictures, books, porcelain—and
that, in his line of business, he would know how to
make the best of. But he hadn't taken any of them,
as far as I could tell. He would scarcely have had
time to. And in any case, if that was what he wanted
it didn't make sense to behave as he had just done. If
he wanted the valuable stuff, he had two alternatives: the legal one, of contesting the will and hoping for the best, and the illegal one, of organising a

house-breaking: an efficient one, not a bungled attempt.

So if it was not the antiques he was after, then it must be something in the nature of a document, a letter, diaries, something that his aunt possessed that could connect him with the car driven over my wife over a year ago. Something that he knew Miranda had, and that she knew the significance of, and that had caused her, because she could not quite bring herself to betray her nephew, to leave all her possessions to me.

Or had she perhaps in leaving me the house with its contents, hoped that I would find this piece of evidence among my inheritance and realise what it meant and pursue her nephew to retribution? It was this last supposition that made the tone go wrong. It showed up the whole thing as too easy, too neat. I had built up in my mind a theory based on nothing but a hunch, and then I had used a few facts to build up another theory that fitted in neatly with the first one.

What I ought to do was to shake Imogen's death from my mind and consider my suspicions of Mervyn Porlock purely in the light of what I actually knew about him and his aunt. If I did this, a very different picture might emerge.

But I could not do it. The whole situation was so inextricably linked up with my feeling of coming out of my mourning for Imogen that I simply could not cut the mental connection between the Porlocks and her death.

"I saw the blunt instrument," said Marilyn's voice

in my ear, "and the whole business looks so daft that it just has to be true."

"Of course it's true. I bashed my head against a branch. I told you. Ouch." It was throbbing and very sore, but I was feeling much less giddy now.

"Some head," she said unsympathetically, "and some branch. You've knocked it right out of the tree."

I began to laugh. "The tree's coming to pieces. It's terribly ancient. Did you find the bag of nuts I was going to hang up for the birds?"

"Nuts to you," she said, suddenly producing it from behind her back. "And here are the letters you dropped."

I took the three brown envelopes that I had been carrying round with me since I picked them off the mat after letting myself into Beth's Cottage. Two of them contained circulars; the third was the electricity account. No wonder Mervyn had not bothered to steal them.

"Why did you go out to feed the birds?" asked Marilyn curiously. "What's that got to do with dealing with Miss Porlock's affairs?"

"Oh, I just felt like it. I told you I was daft. It must be the spring. Come on. Let's go."

I stood up too quickly and had to hold on to the back of the chair to steady myself.

"Don't you want to pick up any letters or documents or anything?" asked Marilyn as I began to move rather shakily towards the door. "There's some stuff here in this little desk," she went on. "It's in a frightful mess. But isn't it pretty? The desk, I mean. Is it rosewood?"

"I suppose I'd better have a look," I said. "I'm not really expecting to find anything, though."

She gave me a keen look and then shook her head and shrugged as if to say that my whole attitude and behaviour was quite beyond her understanding. I felt too ashamed to confess to her that I had not yet examined the desk. Rapidly I shuffled through the papers lying on top and in the drawers, but it was more to please Marilyn than because I really wanted to look just now. My reluctance was partly rational, because obviously the search would tell me nothing about what Mervyn had been looking for, and partly irrational, because I did not want to upset my own theory any further. If Mervyn had found what he wanted, then it would most certainly no longer be in Beth's Cottage, but if I let myself think too closely about what he might have been looking for. . . .

There were accounts and receipts in the drawers, a number of circulars, an estimate for repairs to the roof, catalogues of art exhibitions, old theatre programmes, reviews of books cut from newspapers. No personal letters; no photographs.

"No will," said Marilyn in a disappointed voice.

"It would seem not."

I answered lightly, but underneath I felt a sickening sense of flatness and anticlimax which was not entirely due to the throbbing in my head.

No will. But of course there had been a will. That was what Mervyn had come for. It was as simple as that. He knew that his aunt had made a will in his favour, although he had pretended to me that she had made none. He believed he would find it in her desk, and it had been a great shock to him to learn that she had revoked it and made another will on her deathbed. The circumstances were such that he had high hopes of proving this last will invalid, but his case would be strengthened if he could produce the earlier will, rather than try to prove that she had died intestate.

If he had found me friendly and co-operative he might have confided in me and sought my help. I had been just the opposite, and it was his suspicions of me that had led him to such drastic measures. He'd guessed that I had benefitted under the deathbed will, and he suspected me of trying to destroy the earlier one. He must have watched me through the window from wherever he was hiding in the grounds. Had I shown signs of destroying any papers, no doubt he would have rushed in and challenged me. As it was, I did nothing but look around and come out to feed the birds, and that gave him his chance to get into the house.

A stupid, arrogant thing to do, but then, he was a stupid and arrogant man. And the gamble had paid off, because I had been stupid and careless. He had his will and would try to prove it, but I would be very hard put to prove that he had knocked me on the head in order to obtain it.

It made sense. Not a false note anywhere. All to do with Mervyn's desire not to lose his inheritance and nothing whatsoever to do with Imogen's death. My mind alone had connected the two. Of course there was still the fact that Miss Porlock had at the last moment made me her heir, but no doubt one of the other reasons I had put forward for that would prove the true one after all.

"I think I'd better sit down again for a while," I said to Marilyn. "I'm still feeling rather giddy."

But it was not only giddiness; it was disappointment. And disgust with myself for being so carried away by my fantasies that I had not thought of this far more likely explanation for Mervyn's behaviour and, worst of all, that I had let him get away with it.

Marilyn was standing over me, looking rather worried. "Perhaps I could make some tea or something," she said. "Would it be all right to use the kitchen? I mean, I have the feeling that we ought not to be here."

I knew what she meant. As we ate our little meal of tinned soup and cheese and biscuits, I, too, had the feeling that we were trespassers. Marilyn chatted about Miss Porlock, trying to get me to tell her exactly what had happened the previous evening. I parried her questions.

"But even if we find a will here," she said, "it won't matter, because she made a new one yesterday."

"How did you know that? I never told you."

"Jenny told me. She took the message from the hospital yesterday afternoon when I was on the other line."

It was obvious that I was not going to be able to keep my inheritance a secret from my colleagues for much longer. In fact, for all I knew, Geoff might have discovered about it already. He held the other key to the office safe, and if he saw the envelope and was feeling curious . . . after all, we shared the work and consulted each other over everything. You can't keep things to yourself in a small law office. Not when they take the form of vital legal documents signed by clients of the firm. And in any case, Mervyn Porlock would soon be getting busy and all would have to be revealed. Very much so.

The thought of a long-drawn-out public wrangle over the will made my heart quail, but I could see no alternative. Of course I could give all the assets away if I wanted to, and probably in the end I would do so, but first of all it had to be proved that they were mine to give. That was the task entrusted to me by Miranda. The only way to get out of carrying out that task was to take the law into my own hands, in the style of Mervyn Porlock, and destroy the document that lay in the office safe.

Marilyn was asking me outright what had happened at the hospital.

"You'll know soon enough," I replied. "Miss Porlock has made a perfectly valid will—at least I think it is—and it's going to be a damned nuisance."

Her eyes lit up. "Damned nuisances" of cases usually made quite interesting work for the secretaries and clerks.

"We're not acting for Mr. Porlock, are we?" she asked.

"Certainly not."

"But against him?"

"Very probably."

She gave a little cheer.

"Male chauvinist pig or not," I said, "do you think you could clear these things away into the kitchen now, because we ought to be getting back to the office. God knows what's been happening about all those matters you were supposed to be dealing with."

"Oh. Brenda said she'd cope."

This didn't reassure me at all. "Did you ring Mrs. Perkins and tell her the completion date?"

"Yes, and I rang the Town Hall about the rates and—oh gosh!" exclaimed Marilyn suddenly, interrupting herself.

"Well? And what sin of omission has just come into your mind?"

We both knew that she had been forgiven even before she confessed. In any case, whatever minor detail she had missed could not even begin to approach my own sins of omission. In fact, for the sake of my reputation as a responsible professional man, my activities over the past few hours were best forgotten. It turned out that Marilyn's slip was even more trivial than I had anticipated.

"I made all the urgent calls," she said, "but I've only just remembered that I was supposed to give you this."

She was rummaging in her handbag as she spoke, and eventually unearthed a small white envelope. I took it from her and saw that it had my name on it in her own handwriting.

"Someone brought it in about half an hour after you'd left the office," she said.

I hardly heard her. I had opened the envelope and taken out a small piece of paper with the Queen Mary Hospital letterhead. Stapled to this was an even smaller piece of paper, which on examination turned out to be half of an old envelope containing part of an address: Miss M. Porlock, Beth's Cottage.

The rest was torn away, but in the space left above the address, to the left of the postmark, were some words in a handwriting that I instantly recognised to be that of Miranda herself.

"Rosemary—emerald ring?" I read. And beneath that: "Andy. Books. Picture?"

I stared at these words in a silence that lasted too long for Marilyn's patience.

"Is it important?" she asked. "She said it could wait till you got back to the office."

"Sorry," I said, returning the enclosure to the envelope. "My thought processes still seem to be rather lethargic. Important? I don't know yet. I'll have to find out more about it. Who did you say delivered this, Marilyn?"

"A woman. She seemed to be in rather a hurry. She didn't say what it was about or anything. Just wanted you to have it when you got back."

I didn't think Marilyn had seen the heading of the paper. As far as she knew, it could be concerned with quite a different matter, and I didn't want to reveal by my behaviour that it had to do with the Porlock case, although I was longing to know whether it was Grace herself who had brought the letter, and if so, what was Marilyn's impression of her.

"That's all right," I said. "It's certainly not urgent."

I shut the front door of Beth's Cottage behind us, and we walked down the path between the daffodils. At the gate I said casually: "What sort of a woman? How about one of your lightning character sketches?"

She looked pleased and then frowned. "It's difficult."

"Marilyn Godley admit defeat!" I laughed at her. "Come on, girl, have a shot at it."

"She looked the sort of person you feel you'd like to get to know but who might not be easy to get to know," she said at last.

This was interesting, though not quite up to Marilyn's usual standard of pithy comment. However, it was enough to make me feel sure that it had been Grace herself, and a few enquiries about her appearance bore this out. I had actually stopped asking questions and had taken a step towards the car when Marilyn, evidently sensing that her reputation was at stake, said something that really did surprise me and set me thinking.

"She looked sort of . . . haunted. No, that's too strong. Just rather worried perhaps. Maybe a bit scared. I think she was disappointed that you weren't there."

I fished in my pocket for the car keys and made no reply. Haunted? Worried? Scared? This was not my image of the doctor who had shown me such wisdom and compassion, but it bore out my suspicion that her calmness was only maintained by a great effort of self-discipline. Grace with the mask down. Young Marilyn had caught a glimpse of what lay behind the mask. Was I to be permitted more than a glimpse when she came to see me on the morrow? And she had "seemed disappointed" not to see me.

It seemed safest not to let myself dwell on this remark at all. Marilyn was much too bright and observant and inquisitive and I should certainly give myself away.

"Are you sure you're fit to drive?" she asked as I opened the car door.

"Probably not. I'll go very slowly and you'll drive behind me and if you think I'm about to pass out you must hoot loudly."

She laughed and waved as she got into Jenny's mini, and I knew that we were safely back in our normal roles again.

I felt very grateful to Marilyn as we made our way carefully back to Swanhurst. She had brought me through a nasty, troublesome hour, and I was very glad indeed that she had taken the initiative of coming. But she was too young and too raw to be my confidante. Talk to someone I must before very long, because I was in such a volatile and emotional state that my judgement was not to be trusted, but it must be someone much more experienced and mature than Marilyn.

It must be Grace, who already knew so much about my affairs that it was silly to try to keep from her the essence of Miranda's will. In any case, she had probably guessed the truth, and she would bring her balanced common sense to my see-saw of speculation. That she had taken the trouble to bring the memo written by Miss Porlock to me at the office was evidence of her interest in the matter. And perhaps—I dared to think this now that I was alone in my car and safe from Marilyn's keen eye—perhaps it was also evidence of some personal interest in myself.

Haunted, worried, and perhaps even afraid. Marilyn had admitted to exaggerating in her desire to impress me with her own perceptiveness. And there are very many people who, when the defences are momentarily down, reveal some private desperation. Faces in a rush-hour crowd, the faces of drivers in a traffic snarl-up or on wet and foggy nights—you don't need to go far to see the sort of thing that Marilyn had described. But nevertheless, after making all allowances, I was still left with the sense that Dr. Grace Watson had some great undigested grief of her own, which gave her exceptional understanding of other people's troubles.

I longed to be able to help her, as she had helped me. We had met over a deathbed and had in some strange way received a blessing from the dying woman. That was a great bond between us. And perhaps there was another bond as well. If Miranda Porlock's end had set off some process within me, might it not have done the same for Grace? The thawing out of frozen feelings could be a rather alarming business, and might well account for the look upon which Marilyn had based her judgement.

CHAPTER 5

My encounter with an apple tree made a good story in the office. Everybody was sympathetic and very ready with their advice on what I should do with my sore head, but there was a strong undercurrent of amusement present as well. I was, after all, chief in my little domain, and however well disposed they are towards him, people always like to have a tale to tell about the boss. My reputation for being impulsive and somewhat absent-minded would be much enhanced by the tale of the tree.

If they had known that I had actually been attacked . . . but no, that would be going too far. There is a limit to the amount of eccentricity permissible in the senior partner of a little local law firm.

As soon as I was left in peace, I telephoned the hospital. Dr. Watson was not available, but Sister Jenkins came on the line. Yes, she was only too pleased to tell me about the piece of paper that had been found stuck in the drawer of the locker by Miss Porlock's bed. In fact she had found it herself; apparently it had been overlooked by the nurse who was supposed to collect Miss Porlock's things together.

"I thought it might be important," went on Sister Jenkins, "so I told Dr. Watson about it, and she agreed and said you ought to have it straight away, but we had no one to send. So as I can't leave the ward, and in any case I don't drive a car, she said she would come herself, since it would only take ten minutes or so."

"It was very good of her, very good of you both. As you've probably guessed, Sister, I think there may well be some trouble over the will you witnessed, and anything that might help to establish Miss Porlock's wishes may be of use. This looks to me as if she was jotting down her ideas for disposing of her estate."

"That's what it looked like to me," said the ward sister in a satisfied tone of voice, and I decided to get Grace to tell Sister Jenkins the whole story too. After all, if it came to a fight with Mervyn Porlock over my inheritance, these two, the doctor and the nurse, would be vital witnesses, and they were going to such trouble to help me that I felt more and more mean for not having taken them into my confidence before. The fact that the ward sister was clearly enjoying the drama of it did not make me any less grateful to her.

"Miss Porlock's nephew has been here," she went on. "We thought you'd like to know that, too. He's not been gone very long."

"When did he arrive?"

"Oh . . . an hour or more ago."

The times fit in, I thought. That would mean he drove straight from Mill Green to the hospital.

"He wanted to know all about his aunt's death," said Sister Jenkins.

"Did you tell him what happened?"

"Exactly what happened."

"Good. I'm sorry you are having all this trouble. I'm afraid you haven't heard the last of it yet."

"Oh, that's all right," said Sister Jenkins. "It makes a change from the usual routine."

"Then, I wonder if I could trouble you with just one more question. I wonder if you could run your mind back over the period when Miss Porlock was in your care and try to remember any little incident, anything at all, however trivial, that seemed to indicate some sort of change in her. I don't mean a medical change, but some sort of change in attitude, in her behaviour. Did she ever seem to become agitated, or angry, or anything like that, and if so, can anybody remember what was happening to her at the time? Apart from the medical tests and treatments. I know this is not an easy thing to ask. I know she was extremely ill and that you were trying to save her and to make her comfortable, but if anybody can remember anything along the lines I have suggested, then I'd be most grateful to know."

"I'll talk to the others," said Sister Jenkins, "and we'll do our best."

After we had rung off, I rather wished I'd asked her what to do about my sore head, but decided it was better not to: She'd only tell me to come to hospital, and I still had a lot I wanted to get through before I gave in and rested it. I made photocopies of Miss Porlock's will and set the usual procedures in motion. From the cheque-book in the handbag, I learnt the name of her bank and made an appointment to see the manager the next day. Then I made arrangements with a local firm about valuing Beth's

Cottage and its contents. Marilyn, typing my letters, had of course to learn that I was Miranda's heir, but I begged her to keep quiet about it for today. Just let me get over the bump on my head, I said, before I had to face the curiosity of my colleagues.

But, shortly before five o'clock, I changed my mind and decided that I would have to tell Geoff about it. In fact I ought to have told him earlier. Perhaps it was not simply that I had not had much chance to do so, but that I felt too embarrassed. Rich, lonely old ladies do sometimes leave money to their solicitors, just as they do to their doctors or nurses or housekeepers. And why not? In their position I would rather reward a paid professional who carried out the job well and eased my body and mind than leave my money to a relative who didn't really care what happened to me. In any case, I intended to give all Miranda's money away, keeping only the house for myself.

Geoff had been the beneficiary of such legacies. No single one as big as mine, but in all they had added up to a considerable sum, and as far as I knew, he never gave anything away. So why should I be embarrassed? Was it because Miss Porlock had originally been his client? She could have continued to be, and maybe he would have reaped the lot, had he not shifted the job onto me because it was a tiresome overtime chore that he wanted to avoid. Or was it that there was a sort of rivalry between us, inevitable perhaps with an older partner coming near to retirement and the younger one looking forward to taking over and doing things differently?

I went up to his room to tell him. It was a pleasant

room, on the first floor, above my own office. People sometimes wonder why I did not take the room for myself, but actually I preferred to be downstairs, at the centre of things. He was signing letters, with Brenda whipping them away and shoving them into the envelopes as soon as he had done. The rush to get away from the office in good time was already starting, and here was poor old Harry, who didn't care how late he worked, coming along to make a nuisance of himself just at this moment.

I could feel them both thinking this.

"I shall keep you exactly five minutes," I said to Geoff when he had finished and Brenda had dashed downstairs to the franking machine.

"Oh, that's all right, old man." He tried hard to look as if he didn't mind if I kept him for fifty. Perhaps that's what is the matter with Geoffrey Holdsworth. He tries too hard to project the perfect image all the time. "How's the head?" he added.

"About the same. I'm taking it home to nurse it shortly, but I must tell you this first." I hurried on to prevent him from feeling that he had to make sympathetic noises about my headache or offer to drive me to the hospital or come home with me, or anything tiresome or inconvenient like that. "Miranda Porlock left me her whole estate. Crazy, isn't it?"

After I had briefly outlined the events of the previous evening, Geoffrey said, without expression, "Next of kin?"

"Nephew. He was here in the office today. He'll fight it. Look, don't let's waste time speculating—you want to get home, and so do I. All I want to know is, can you remember anything Miss Porlock said when

she came to see you last autumn? There's nothing at
all on the file. You said you interviewed her and she
had one of those vague stories about neighbours per-
secuting her or something. But Geoff, she hasn't got
any neighbours. There are beech woods all round
the house. The nearest dwelling is a farm, quite a
long way back from the road."

"Sorry if I misled you," replied Geoff. "No, it
wasn't exactly neighbours. It was some sort of
ramblers club, as far as I remember, who were
claiming there was an old footpath going up into the
woods alongside her garden. The old girl had been
visited by a couple of hippie types who had put the
wind up her."

"Really? She didn't seem to me the sort who'd
scare easily."

"Well, maybe she wasn't so much scared. Agitated, rather. Not wanting her privacy invaded. I
remember she talked a lot about her privacy. And I
remember I was privately wondering whether they
were anything to do with a ramblers club at all, or
whether they were on the look-out for antiques or
something. Old lady on her own, valuable stuff in the
attic. That sort of thing."

"It's the sort of house where that could happen," I
admitted. "But nothing more came of it?"

"Not as far as I know. She wanted to know the
law about rights of way, and I must say she was no
fool. We left it that she should get in touch if anything else happened. Presumably it didn't. From
what you say, I'd guess it was someone casing the
joint and then changing their minds."

"You don't think she was casing our joint?"

"Come again?" Geoff looked puzzled.

"I mean, could she have used this story as an excuse to have a look at us and decide whether she'd like us to handle her affairs for her?"

Geoff laughed. "Too subtle for me, old man. I like to deal in facts, not speculations."

I was irritated by this remark. Geoff was just as fond of theorising as anybody else. More so, on occasion. But he really was riled, as I'd known he would be, by the fact that Miss Porlock's estate had not come to him. If only he would say so openly and admit that he was annoyed with himself for passing on the job to me! Any minute now he would be pretending he'd handed it on to me because he'd thought it might cheer me up.

"Thanks anyway," I said quickly to avoid having to talk to Geoff any more about the matter now. "I'm off home. It's more than time I laid my aching head on a pillow."

"Well, if there's anything I can do—"

"I'll let you know. Cheers, Geoff."

For the first time since Imogen's death, I was really glad to leave the office. When I got home, I didn't even trouble to put the car in the garage, but left it in the drive. Then I swallowed some aspirin and lay down and slept for about an hour and a half. When I woke, the headache was still there and I felt very feeble, but the feverishness that had carried me through the afternoon's activities had left me. So had the feeling of nausea, and I was very hungry.

I ate up everything I could find that didn't need much doing to it, drank quantities of sweet tea, made a mental note that I must replenish the food stocks tomorrow since Grace was coming to dinner, and sat and thought for a while. It was not yet dark and there was still some of the evening left and I didn't feel like going to bed for another couple of hours. Neither did I feel like reading or music or any of my usual solitary pastimes. What I would have liked most in the world was to talk to Grace, but that would have to wait for twenty-four hours. The next-best thing would be to see Beth's Cottage again. One of the great advantages of being on your own is that you can do things that other people regard as rash or silly or inadvisable without having to argue and defend yourself.

As I packed an overnight case, I could hear young Marilyn's protesting voice in my mind. It didn't affect my decision, but it did make me think that I ought to let somebody know where I was. Supposing Mervyn were to strike again, or supposing those hippie-type ramblers of many months ago really were prospecting housebreakers? My neighbours and I kept an eye on each other's property and told each other if we were going to be away. Fortunately they were out for the evening, so there was no need for any personal contact. I left a note in their letter-box and for the second time that day drove up the lane where Imogen had died.

Friday, the twenty-first of March, at about three-thirty in the afternoon, last year. Supposing Mervyn had been visiting his aunt and was driving back to London. He would have to come through Swanhurst, and if he knew the town and its environs at all, he would know that this was the best way. He would be an aggressive and selfish driver. Just the sort of person to knock someone down and not stop. After all, he'd knocked me out and left me. Suppose I'd been badly hurt? Suppose Marilyn had not come in search of me? And suppose—since I was indulging in this orgy of speculation instead of sticking to facts—that he hadn't knocked me out just because he wanted to get into the house but because he wanted me out of the way.

Mervyn had run down Imogen. All right, so in law it was not a terribly serious offence: A fine, the driving licence taken away—these were the sort of penalties that would be given to whoever could be proved to have killed my wife. But it is not only the law. There is still such a thing as public opinion and public reputation, and to a man like Mervyn this would be very important, apart from the fact that it would be very inconvenient for him to lose his licence.

Mervyn would certainly not want it made public if he was indeed the culprit. If he knew that I was on his track he might well try to get rid of me. I hardly thought he would go so far as trying to kill me, but he might try to put me out of action for a while, or frighten me off my search. Particularly if he was at very little risk of discovery. And Beth's Cottage was an isolated house, with a very secluded garden. Nobody ever came there except the postman, and he not very frequently.

Deep in this not very comforting train of thought, I drove past Beth's Cottage and on into the village of Mill Green. It was quite dark now, but, oddly enough, the place looked more alive and welcoming by night than by day. Lights shone in porches and in cottage windows, and the Plough Inn, which was my destination, actually looked quite bright and cheerful.

I went into the bar, and then immediately wished I had not come. Not that there was anything wrong with the place. On the contrary. It was peaceful and old-fashioned. Genuinely so, not reconstituted period. And the few people there, mostly middle-aged, looked like genuine locals.

My difficulty was that I had not thought how to present myself. Did I pretend to be a complete stranger, passing through Mill Green just this once and never again? Hardly, since I proposed to make the village my home and I was bound to meet these people again. Should I, then, go to the other extreme and say straight out that I had a professional interest in the late Miss Porlock and would like to know what the village thought of her? That might set the tongues wagging. Or it might have the opposite effect. In the end I decided to feel my way.

"I'm on the way to Beth's Cottage," I said to an elderly couple who sat down near to me, "and I can't help wondering who the original 'Beth' was."

Neither of them knew, and they doubted whether anybody else would either. They had lived in Mill Green for ten years and never heard the cottage called anything else.

"There's an old woman living there now," said the husband. "Bit of a recluse. Miss Pollard? Pollitt?"

"Porlock," corrected his wife. "I don't know her other name. Maybe she is called Beth."

I was just registering the fact that this couple, at any rate, did not know that Miranda Porlock was dead, when they plunged me into a fresh quandary.

"And maybe our friend here already knows that," said the man, "since he's on the way to visit."

"Well, it's not exactly a social visit," I said hurriedly. "More in the line of business, you know. Bit late in the evening to be doing business, but sometimes we have to."

This idiotic remark provoked the puzzled looks that it deserved. They murmured something politely and I suddenly felt I could not bear to go blundering on like this, getting the worst of both worlds, creating a bad impression and yet learning nothing.

"I don't know if you knew Miss Porlock at all," I said in a much firmer voice, "but if so, then I'm afraid it's bad news. She died in hospital in Swanhurst a few days ago. I am dealing with her estate and I've come to have a look at the house. Johnson's my name."

"Grant," said the man. "No, we didn't know her at all. She never came in here, nor called on anyone. And she didn't go to church, or do any shopping in the village. In fact I don't even know how we knew her name. How did we know her name, Elsie?"

"Through Dr. Freeman," was the prompt reply.

A doctor? I pricked up my ears. Perhaps, after all, I was to find out something about Miss Porlock. Maybe I was to learn the identity of the "Andy" to whom she had been thinking of leaving her books and perhaps a picture. But it turned out that Dr. Freeman had once been called to Beth's Cottage not for Miss Porlock but for a man who was lopping down a diseased elm tree near to the house and had fallen off the ladder. It had happened many months before, and Dr. John Freeman, an elderly, semi-

retired general practitioner, had since died. The injured young man had been working for the local
council, and my couple knew nothing more about
him and apparently cared less.

Miss Porlock's death, however, was news. Not
even the barmaid had heard about it. One often
hears it said that everybody always knows everybody else's business in a small village, but this evening seemed to be disproving this particular item of
folk wisdom. People had seen Miss Porlock occasionally, and some had even spoken to her, but all
they could say of her was that she was an odd-look-
ing woman and appeared to want to keep herself to
herself. It seemed very sad, but what could one do?
Nobody, apparently, had ever seen Mervyn or even
knew of his existence. His visits to his aunt must
have been even rarer than I had supposed.

With such a dearth of matter for discussion, the
subject of Miss Porlock was soon exhausted, and after Mrs. Grant had hoped that somebody would take
over Beth's Cottage who would be more friendly towards the neighbourhood, the talk shifted to a road-
widening scheme that would involve cutting down
two of the old chestnut trees on the village green.
Everybody became very excited about this, and in
the course of the discussion it turned out that Mr.
Grant was a footpath enthusiast.

"Isn't there supposed to be an old right of way up
the hill in the woods alongside Beth's Cottage?" I
asked, suddenly remembering what Geoff had told
me.

"Never heard of any," said Mr. Grant decisively.
"The land belongs to the Allison Estate. The cottage

must have been some sort of gamekeeper's lodge at one time or another."

"Then, I must be thinking of some other property," I said, and hurried on to ask some other questions about the neighbourhood before getting up to go.

I had been the best part of an hour in the bar, consumed several drinks that I did not want at all, and apart from the very faint possibility that the young man employed by the local council to cut down diseased elm trees was the "Andy" of Miss Porlock's memo, I had learnt nothing. Miranda was as great a mystery as ever. Her reputation as a recluse was amply confirmed, but as far as I could judge, any suspicions of her neighbours were ill-founded. It didn't look as if anybody had been thrusting his friendship on her. She had wanted to be let alone, and let alone she had been, except by the young men who wanted to open up a footpath. But since Mr. Grant looked the sort of man who would never make a mistake about his hobby, it rather looked as if the incident related by Geoff had been some sort of hoax or attempted confidence trick.

Unless Miss Porlock had made up the story herself and it was Geoff who had been taken in. One does have clients from time to time who come along with tales that turn out to be completely untrue. I was feeling irritable and frustrated as I got back to my car, and when I felt a hand grab at my sleeve and a young man's voice say, "Hi—d'you want to know something?" I snapped back.

"Yes. I want to know everything. I suppose you are in a position to tell me?"

He was a tall boy with long, matted fair hair and a shy expression behind the awkwardness. He had been sitting with a girl at the far end of the bar, the only young people in the place.

"Sorry," he muttered, going very red in the face. "I couldn't help hearing, and I thought maybe—"

Hastily I apologised for my quite uncalled-for sarcasm.

"Are you a detective?" he asked.

"No, but I very much want to find out more about Miss Porlock. For personal reasons. If you can tell me anything, no matter how trivial, I should be very glad to hear."

"Well, I don't suppose it's anything really, but I work at the farm and sometimes when I've been bringing the tractor round I've seen a car stopping at her house."

"A white car?" Could he possibly have seen Mervyn?

"No. A black car. Looks like a taxi."

A taxi. Of course. Miranda would have had to get about somehow. She had actually had the heart attack in the public gardens in Swanhurst. There was no bus service to Mill Green, and she certainly would not have been able to walk all the way from the village to the town. Besides, she would have had to do her shopping somewhere else if she never went into the village shop or had anything delivered.

A taxi. Of course. And where there was a taxi there must be a driver, and people talk a lot to taxi-drivers; it's a sort of moving confessional, as if one were in limbo, and secrets can be safely revealed. I felt my heart warm to the clumsy-looking farm lad and wished I could think of an adequate way to thank him.

"You never spoke to Miss Porlock yourself?" I asked.

He shook his head. "Nothing to say to her," he muttered.

Here was one of that very rare breed who only speak when they have something to say, and I had snubbed him most unkindly. I felt bad about that.

"I'm very grateful to you indeed," I said. "Do you mind if I ask you one thing more? Have you seen any other cars stopping at Beth's Cottage? At any time, but particularly this afternoon."

"Not this afternoon. I've been in the long fields— other side of the hill. At any other time?" He thought a moment. "The mail van maybe. Can't think of anything else. Except the black car."

"Is it a local taxi? I mean, does anybody here, in Mill Green, run a service?"

"No, but I'm thinking of starting one," he said with a sudden friendly smile. "Nice clean work, better money than drilling barley. But where do I get the two thousand pounds from?"

"Don't despair," I said. "It may come your way. What's your name?"

"Paul."

"Paul," I repeated, and added to myself: Not Andy, but then, I never expected this boy to be the one named in the memo. "I know where to find you. I'm going to be around Mill Green quite a lot in future and I could well be interested in a taxi service. Thanks again."

As I drove away, I decided that those people who

accused me of being crazily impulsive were right after all. Paul should have his two thousand pounds. Anybody who helped me solve my mystery should have anything he or she wanted.

Taxis. That was something definite to go on at last, but it would have to wait until tomorrow. Meanwhile here was Beth's Cottage, all in the dark but I would soon remedy that. The car would have to stay on the patch of grass outside the hedge.

I took my flashlight from the car, but I must confess it was with some nervousness that I approached the house. It was very dark and very lonely and very quiet, except for faint rustlings of leaves and twigs. It was a relief to get inside and turn on all the lights. I left them burning, and went round all the doors and windows on the ground floor, making everything as secure as I could.

Then I went upstairs. I had decided to stay in the room Miranda had been using. I would not actually go to bed, because I wanted to be dressed and ready in case anything should happen, but I could rest and doze there, and even sleep if I were undisturbed.

I left the window uncovered because I wanted to wake to the sight of the beech trees and the song of the birds. Half of me was back in my sentimental dream; the other half was cautious and a little apprehensive.

It was the latter part that glanced around the room and had quite a shock. Everything looked exactly as it had looked that afternoon except in one respect: The big studio portrait of Mervyn that his aunt had only partially unwrapped was no longer there. I moved aside the other photographs on top of the linen chest, raised the lid, and looked inside. There was a jumble of old clothes, cushion covers, coat-hangers, bits of wrapping paper, and other assorted household rubbish, but no photographs. I rummaged in the chest for several minutes but found nothing of interest.

Nor did the photograph appear to be anywhere else in the room. In my search I came across a lot more worn and shabby articles as well as clothes that were old-fashioned but good, and some old-fashioned jewellery. Why didn't Mervyn take these rings and brooches? I wondered; nobody would ever have known he had done so.

Perhaps they were too trivial, not worth the notice of such a high-class international consultant for the antiques trade.

Then, why take away the photograph of himself? It didn't seem to make any sense at all. All I could suppose was that, having found the earlier will or whatever it was that he was prepared to knock me on the head for, he had then suddenly decided that he might as well have the photograph back, rather than waste it. It was not perhaps a very rational thing to do, even for such a vain person as Mervyn, but then, human beings so very often do act irrationally, particularly when they are in a state of anxiety and agitation. And after all, I hadn't been behaving all that sensibly myself.

CHAPTER 6

Nothing occurred to disturb my rest until the first bird song at dawn. I washed and helped myself to some more of the contents of the fridge and the store cupboard, and then I walked out into the orchard to feed the finches—successfully this time. After that, I inspected the apple tree. There was, as Marilyn had said, quite a substantial piece of rough loose wood fallen down among the low-hanging boughs. What I could not find was any spot on the tree from which it could recently have broken off, and I wondered whether Marilyn had looked closely too and formed her own suspicions.

I hoped not, because I proposed to spend a lot of time in the house, and I didn't want her or anybody else fussing over me. I loved Beth's Cottage as much as ever and would gladly have spent the whole day there, lying on the bed or in a deck-chair, strolling round the garden, or just sitting and looking at the greenfinches and the blue tits and at the leaves moving in the sunlight.

I was as if born anew. The terrible thing about bereavement, or any other intense depression, is that it takes absolutely everything away from you. Not only is there this enormous black yawning hole within you, but all the real world outside has altered too.

Flowers lose their colour and music loses its melody and food loses its flavour and friends lose their humanity because there is nothing in you to respond to the humanity in them.

My hole was still there, but the other blessings were being restored to me, all the sweeter for their long absence.

"You'd have loved this place, Imogen," I said aloud.

Before I left, I had one more look at the desk in the living-room. Even if, as it seemed, Miranda Porlock had destroyed the few personal letters that she received, she must surely have had some sort of address book. All I could find was a short list of telephone numbers written on the back of an old envelope and tucked into the front of the telephone directory. Police, a plumber, Mervyn's London number, Dr. Freeman—that's out of date, I thought, remembering last night's chat at the Plough Inn. Then came the name "Rosemary," followed by another London number. Rosemary. One of the names on the memo. This was the first clue I had received to any personal relationship other than with Mervyn, and it looked as if it was quite a close tie, since Miss Porlock had noted the name when she was about to make her will. Probably she had been intending to add other names to receive other small bequests, but when it came to the point, she had had strength only to dictate the one simple clause. I made a note of the telephone number. Perhaps this lady would be able to help me, and in any case she should have her souvenir.

The next entry also interested me: It was "Solici-

tor," and my office number in Swanhurst followed.
But the last item on the list was the most useful for
my present purposes. It said "Taxi," and alongside
was written another telephone number in Swanhurst.

This could save me a great deal of time and effort.
In the local telephone directory there was a large
number of entries under the heading "Taxis and
Hire Cars," and I might have had to go through most
of them before I tracked down Miss Porlock's driver,
or drivers. I was so pleased with my discovery that I
decided to ring the number straight away. A girl's
voice answered.

"Country Cabs. Can I help you?"

"Yes, please. I'm ringing on behalf of a customer
of yours: Miss Miranda Porlock. Do you recollect the
name?"

The voice did recollect the name. "Excuse me a
moment," it added. I heard voices over the wire but
could distinguish no words. Then the girl returned.
"Sorry about that, but we were just talking about
Miss Porlock and wondering what had happened to
her, since we hadn't had a call this week."

"I'm sorry to say that Miss Porlock is dead. She
died in hospital two days ago."

"Oh, dear." The voice sounded genuinely upset,
and it suddenly struck me that in all these hours
since Miranda's death, this was the first indication I
had received that anybody cared. Her only mourner:
a car-hire firm. Well, I suppose there are some people who die without leaving even that much regret
behind them.

I explained that I was Miss Porlock's solicitor and

that I particularly wanted to get in touch with whoever had driven the taxi that she used. As I spoke, it
occurred to me that it sounded as if I was about to
announce that she had left them a legacy. All right.
So be it. Paul should have his two thousand pounds.
Country Cabs—or rather, the one or more of their
drivers most closely involved with the deceased—
should receive their due. And the Friends of the
Queen Mary Hospital should not be forgotten. By
the time I had added a few more names to the list, I
should be well on the way to getting rid of the
money I did not want.

"Would you like to speak to Andy?" asked the
girl. "He's here in the office now, asking about Miss
Porlock. She always asked for him and he always
drove her if he was free."

Andy. I gave a sort of mental cheer. How gratify-
ing it is when a piece drops neatly into place!

Andy had a young voice, and he, too, sounded
genuinely distressed.

"I knew something was wrong," he said several
times. "I knew she hadn't just dropped us and gone
to somebody else."

I explained my position and added that although
he had not actually been mentioned in her will,
there was strong evidence that she wanted him to
have some of her possessions.

"Well, I did sometimes wonder," he said. "We
were—sort of friends, Miss Porlock and me."

I liked the voice and I liked this answer. He had
had his hopes, naturally enough, but he was no hyp-
ocrite; he didn't pretend surprise.

"There may be quite a long delay," I said, "because there are certain difficulties over her will, but meanwhile I should very much like to meet you. I think you may be able to help me. Are you free at all today?"

There was a consultation at the other end of the line and we fixed that he should come to my office later in the morning, as soon as he got back from driving a client to the airport. I thanked him and replaced the receiver with the feeling of having taken a great step forward. Then I rang the Queen Mary Hospital and asked for Sister Jenkins. Sometimes one stroke of luck leads on to another. Sister was off duty, but on hearing my name the nurse told me that they had all been talking about Miss Porlock and trying to remember everything she had said or done during the days when she lay so ill.

"There was just one little thing," concluded the nurse, "but it probably means nothing."

I begged her to let me be the judge of that.

"Well, it was actually on the morning of the day she died. We'd offered her the radio and books and newspapers, but she didn't seem to want to listen to anything or to try to read. But on that morning we found her looking at a newspaper that someone had left on her bedside table: a copy of the *Evening Gazette* from the day before. We thought she must feel a bit brighter, because she'd actually picked it up and was looking at it, and she was certainly more lively on that day."

"So you think it could have been something she read in the paper that caused her to make an effort to do something?"

"It sounds silly," apologised the nurse.

"It sounds very possible," I corrected her, "and I'm most grateful to you all for taking this trouble. Could I ask you something more? When you say Miss Porlock was more lively, do you mean she seemed happier and more hopeful, or do you mean that she was lively because she was agitated and perhaps worried?"

"Oh, she was agitated," said the nurse. "Very agitated. She wanted someone to make phone calls for her. Sister said she'd arrange it, and I think Miss Porlock calmed down a little after that."

I thanked her again and asked her to thank Sister Jenkins for me. Here was my second little stroke of luck. It looked as if it could have been something she read in that local evening paper that had spurred the sick woman into making, or changing, her will, but there was no point in speculating further until I had seen a copy of the paper.

As soon as I got to the office, I asked Marilyn to get hold of one for me. She was bursting to tell me about something that had arrived in the morning's mail and was not at all pleased to be sent on this errand. The letter she wanted to talk about was from a London solicitor. Mervyn had lost no time. They were acting for Mr. Porlock in the matter of the estate of his late aunt, Miss Miranda Porlock, and they understood from their client that I claimed to be in possession of some document purporting to be the last will and testament of the deceased. They wanted to know whether and by what means I proposed to attempt to establish that claim. Meanwhile I was requested to hand over to Miss Porlock's nephew and heir all those of her possessions that had been in the hospital and that had been handed to me in error by the hospital authorities. Their client was, of course, making the arrangements for the funeral, and it was extremely inconvenient not to have access to her house and possessions.

It was not a very good letter. But then, it must have been very hurriedly composed, and it bore all the marks of somebody trying to make the best of a rather shaky case. There was no telling whether Mervyn had got hold of a will leaving the estate to himself. When Marilyn returned with the newspaper, I dictated a reply, simply setting out the circumstances in which Miss Porlock's last will and testament had been signed and witnessed, and stating that I was applying for probate.

If, I added, their client wished to have any of his aunt's possessions as a souvenir, or if for sentimental or for reasons connected with the funeral he wished to make a visit to the house, then I should be pleased to accompany him.

Marilyn liked this letter, and it put her into a good temper again.

"Are you going to the funeral?" she asked.

"Of course," I replied. "Next Tuesday afternoon. At the crematorium."

Grace Watson had told me this. Mervyn had instructed a local undertaking firm.

Marilyn giggled. "Hadn't we all better come along too, to prevent you fighting a duel with him?"

"I hardly think that will be necessary," I replied in the pompous voice. "It seems quite possible that there will be several other people present."

Country Cabs, most likely; and perhaps the "Rosemary" whose telephone number I would ring later. And perhaps the announcement that would appear in the local paper this evening might produce some more people. I did not think the mortal remains of Miranda Porlock would disappear entirely without notice.

Marilyn left the room, but I had only time to glance at the front-page headline of the old copy of the *Evening Gazette* before Geoff came in and looked over my shoulder.

"Good God, not another air crash!"

"No, it's an old paper." I folded it and put it aside, hoping that he would make no further comment. I can't exactly say that I have ever distrusted Geoff: It's not as strong a feeling as that. Were I not assured of his essential integrity, I would never have taken him as a partner. Yet there is sometimes this uncomfortable feeling between us. We see things differently. I see him as just a bit too slick and he sees me as a quixotic and romantic old dodderer.

He looked gloomy this morning, and when Geoff looks gloomy it is usually for one reason only: his son, Peter.

"What's the trouble this time?" I asked.

"Drugs. Police raid on that mucky dump he's living in."

Last time, it had been squatting in an unoccupied house. Pete had been in the middle of the battle with the bailiffs and had been heavily fined for assault.

"I don't know whether I'm going to be able to keep him out of prison," said Geoff.

I was dying to get on with my own affairs and had

not the slightest desire to hear the sordid details, but Geoff needed to tell me. The "mucky dump" was some sort of communal living arrangement in a seaside town fifteen miles from Swanhurst. Its leading spirit was an aristocratic lady who had identified herself with social "outcasts." She would speak for Peter, and the accent in which she spoke would still carry weight in our class-conscious society. In addition to this asset, Geoff had a colleague in the area who was willing to take on the case and who had been successful in similar cases, and we discussed the possibility of Pete's getting off with a fine or a suspended sentence.

Geoff was in that depressed state of mind when one argues round and round in circles, and I was beginning to despair of the conversation ever coming to an end, when the phone rang and Jenny announced that there was a Mr. Darren come to see me.

"Put him in the waiting-room," I said. "I won't be a moment."

Reluctantly Geoff got up to go.

"I think you've got good reason to be hopeful," I said. "After all, he always makes a good impression, himself. Nobody ever wants to believe that he's guilty."

This was true. Perhaps that was part of the trouble with Peter Holdsworth. He was too easily charming and got away with things far too easily. His father might have been the same had he not been a rigidly conventional person to whom correct appearances were everything. I'm not sneering at Geoff's sort of conformism. For some characters it may be an essential safety net, and the absence of it could lead to a miserable, muddled sort of life like poor Pete's.

I was still thinking about this, and wondering what Grace's opinion would be, when the Country Cabs driver, Andy Darren, came into the room. Why I had expected him to be tall and fair and possibly of a rustic appearance, like the farm lad Paul in the Plough Inn the night before, I really do not know. We seem to make these mental images of people on no evidence whatsoever. In fact Andy was dark and short and neat in navy blue trousers and jacket and roll-necked sweater. It didn't need Marilyn to tell me that here was no male chauvinist pig, but very likely a young man with homosexual tendencies.

It was the "old" look in the young face that brought me to this opinion: the sort of weary and resigned expression that you sometimes see in the eyes of youngsters from oriental lands.

We shook hands and I offered him a cigarette. He accepted, saying: "I don't, really, but I'm nervous."

"And I'm nervous too. Or rather, not so much nervous as excited. I'm very keen to know more about Miss Porlock and I believe you're going to be able to tell me. Am I right?"

For a moment I was afraid I had been too eager. He looked away from me and said, almost defensively: "I liked Miss Porlock."

"So did I," I said.

"But you never knew her."

"Only for a short while. Only when she was dying. But I could tell she had great strength of character. And intelligence."

"She was unusual," said Andy Darren. "We used

to talk about lots of things when I drove her. Including yourself." He glanced at me as he said this and then hastily looked away.

"Myself?" I could not help showing my surprise. "But you didn't know me. Either of you."

"We'd never met you," agreed Andy, "but we knew about you. Because of—because of—" He seemed unable to go on.

"Because of my wife's death?" I said.

He nodded, the dark eyes looking at me anxiously.

"There was quite a bit about it in the local paper," I went on, "but it was more than a year ago. You must have been driving Miss Porlock for a long time."

"Eighteen months ago I first met her. She asked me was I a good driver, and I said, Well, I've had a lot of experience. And she said, I've got a very boring job for you. I want you to wait outside shops in Swanhurst while I do my shopping and then bring me back and carry the stuff into the house. So I said, Very good, madam. And she said, It isn't very good. It's horrible. I hate shopping. So I said she could get most things delivered if she liked, and she said that would be even worse. She couldn't stand people coming to the house. She was sick of people. Her father had been a diplomat and wherever they lived, all over the world, she'd always been expected to entertain people, and then her parents got ill and she nursed them both until they died, and then her brother, who was a widower, got ill and she nursed him, too, and now there was nobody else left of the family but herself and her nephew, and she didn't think much of him—he was in the antiques business and she was sure he was a crook—but she'd loved her brother more than anybody else in the world, so she supposed she'd have to put up with her nephew for his sake."

Andy said all this very quickly, waving his cigarette about and then stubbing it out half smoked.

"You've got an excellent memory," I said. "Did she tell you all this at your first meeting?"

"Oh, yes. And I told her quite a lot too. We got on fine. I'm a Barnardo's boy, by the way," he added with a flash of the defensive manner again.

"Are you?" It seemed wise to show no more than very mild interest. "I think I can understand why you and Miss Porlock took to each other. How often did you drive her to Swanhurst and back?"

"Most weeks, except when I was on holiday or sick. Or there was one of our old clients wanting to be driven to London or the airport."

"I believe you're a very good driver," I said. "Old people feel safe with you."

He smiled and then looked sad. "It's the only thing I know how to do."

"Is it? How about befriending lonely old ladies?"

"Well, I like old ladies."

Better than young ones, I thought. They're safe, they make no sexual demands. They can stand for the mother you never had. Yes indeed, the lonely old recluse and the lonely young orphan had certainly meant quite a lot to each other.

"Did you drive Miss Porlock into Swanhurst on the day she collapsed in the park?" I asked. In fact I was longing to ask about their conversations concerning myself, but the thought that I might be on

the verge of some vital discovery had made me so
agitated again that it seemed safer to clear up some
minor points first.

Andy was eager to tell me about the last time he
had seen Miss Porlock. She had not looked well that
morning, and he'd hoped she was going to see a doctor at last. They did a little shopping, and then she
told him that she wanted to be alone for a while to
try to make up her mind about something important.
He'd thought perhaps she was going to consult a
doctor but didn't want to tell him because she hated
admitting there was anything wrong with her. So he
simply asked where she wanted to be picked up for
the drive back to her home. She said she didn't know
yet, because she'd no idea how long she was going to
be. Andy hadn't known what to say to that. Miss
Porlock always came first with him, but the firm did
have other clients, and he couldn't hang about
indefinitely, even for Miss Porlock. But she had understood his difficulty, and she got him out of it by
saying that as soon as she knew when she wanted to
go home, she'd call in at the office and ask for him.

"But they might have sent me somewhere else,"
he had objected.

She hoped not, she replied, but in that case she'd
have to put up with having another driver this time.

Then she took out a ten-pound note and gave it to
him, and told him to take himself and his friend—
that was the friend he shared a flat with—out to a
meal or a show or something. He'd protested that he
and Miss Porlock would probably be seeing each
other again that afternoon, but she insisted on his

taking the money, just in case this was goodbye for
the time being.

"And it was," said Andy. "It was goodbye for
keeps. I did have to go out on a job, but I told Linda
—that's our receptionist you spoke to—that Miss Porlock would be coming in for a car later that afternoon. When I asked Linda about it next day, she
said she'd never been, and we couldn't understand
it. In the end we decided she must have picked up a
cab in the street somewhere and not bothered to call
us. But it wasn't like her and I wasn't happy about it.
And every day I was expecting her to phone and ask
for me, or at least leave a message, but nothing
came. And the more I thought about it, the more I
felt sure she'd been to a doctor and must be very ill,
but I never thought of hospital. If you hadn't rung
this morning, I was going to go out to her house this
evening and see for myself. I knew she wouldn't be
pleased, but I couldn't stand it any longer, not knowing. I really liked Miss Porlock. I did. I did." The
young man sounded on the verge of tears.

"And she liked you," I said. "She particularly
wanted you to have some of her possessions when
she died. And also some money. That will take some
time to come through, but you can choose something
from the house whenever you like."

This was perhaps rather a rash thing to say, in
view of the uncertainty over the will, but I didn't
care. Andy should have his souvenir, and let Mervyn
Porlock do his worst.

"What would you like?" I asked. "She was thinking of books and perhaps a picture."

"I'd love some books." The dark eyes lit up. "And

I suppose—I suppose I couldn't possibly have her desk?"

"You shall certainly have her desk. I am sure she would have been delighted for you to have it. I can't tell you yet what the money will amount to, because there may well be some difficulties over her estate."

"Her nephew," said Andy promptly.

"Well, yes. I shall do my best, but there're going to be delays."

"It doesn't matter," he said. "I mean, I'll be very glad to have it. But I'm very glad to know she was thinking of me. I do mean that—truly."

"I know you do," I replied, feeling very grateful to the nurses at the Queen Mary Hospital for finding that little piece of paper, and for Grace for having brought it to me. Of course I could always have pretended to Andy that Miss Porlock had remembered him, but it was far better to have a firm basis of evidence for my statement. There was no sign of his defensive manner now, nor of any other symptoms of reserve. I did not believe the young man was mercenary, and I did believe that he had provided the dead woman with true human companionship and that he was sincerely mourning her. But money talks, nevertheless, and the promise of money is a great loosener of tongues. Andy accepted another cigarette and I rang Jenny and Marilyn and told them not to disturb me unless it was really urgent.

Then I said: "Was it you who drove Miss Porlock in to Swanhurst about six months ago?" And I gave him the date of Miranda's interview with Geoff at our office.

He remembered it at once. That was the other occasion when she'd said she was not sure how long she was going to be and she would call the office when she was ready, but that time he had been free to take her home and he picked her up at the shopping centre and she had seemed very unhappy. No, not so much unhappy, but sort of frustrated and worried on the way home. She'd told him she had been hoping to clear up something that was worrying her but it hadn't worked out very well.

So Miranda had been worried and unhappy after the interview with Geoff. Why had it disappointed her? I put careful questions to Andy Darren, testing out the story of the two hippie-type young men and the disused footpath but not giving away the fact that it was to my own office that Miranda had been. Andy's answers gave me a very different picture of what had been concerning Miranda from the picture given by my partner, and I was very much inclined to believe that the young man's version was the truer one. It was not pleasant to feel that Geoff had deliberately misled me, and I tried to tell myself that perhaps his memory was at fault.

Apparently Miranda and Andy had frequently talked about the nature of justice. They liked discussing philosophical abstractions, and she had actually lent him some of her books. But it was not only in the abstract. They often talked about their own lives, deciding that in many ways fate had not been kind to either of them but that they had both come to terms with things and were not unhappy now. It was in the course of one of these talks—for once, Andy's memory failed him and he could not remember exactly when—that my own name had

cropped up. They had both read the report of the
case in the newspaper and agreed that I had been
dealt a heavy blow by fate. They were also agreed
that the driver of the car should have to pay for it in
some way, but Miss Porlock had been the more determined on this point, Andy saying that, as a driver,
he felt sure that the man or woman was already
suffering a great deal from pangs of conscience.

"She said she hoped he was," added Andy, "but
she wished he could suffer even more. She wished
she could find out who did it, and she asked me if I
could do a bit of detective work, me being in the
trade, so to speak, and in a position to find out
things."

"That's very interesting," I said. "That she felt so
strongly about it. After all, it was only a story in the
papers. Nothing to do with her."

"That's what I said, but she said how did I know
it wasn't someone connected with her. Or even
someone connected with me. One of my mates
maybe, and she asked me, if I had suspicions that it
could have been one of our drivers, would I go to
the police. I said I didn't know, that I didn't like the
idea of going to the police and telling on anybody,
and she said that was wrong of me, and we had
quite an argument."

I listened intently. The disturbing emotions with
which I had started the interview were now well
under control and my mind was fully alert.

"So you came to the conclusion that she had some
suspicions of her own about my wife's death," I said
thoughtfully.

"Well, yes," he admitted, "but I don't know that I

ought to be saying this. I mean, I don't want you to feel that—"

"There's no need to worry about me," I interrupted firmly. "It was a terrible blow, but it doesn't upset me to talk about it now. In fact it helps." I hesitated for a moment. Should I tell him that it was not just help in carrying out Miss Porlock's wishes that I wanted, but that my main interest was in fact to discover who had driven the car that killed my wife? Almost immediately I gave myself the answer: There's no need to mention it; he's no fool, he knows it himself.

"Now I'm going to say something that you probably won't believe," I went on. "I would desperately like to know the truth about my wife's death, but if I did know who the driver was, I should be content with just knowing. I should not want to take any action against him. Not now. You don't believe me? No, I can see you don't. But it's true. Even three days ago it would not have been true. But I've changed since then. I agree with you that whoever did it has probably suffered a lot in his mind, and in any case, it wouldn't bring back my wife, would it, whatever I did? Was it one of your mates?"

I shot out this last question in quite a different tone of voice. The boy looked startled, almost frightened. Imogen always used to say that I would have been a good cross-examiner if I hadn't been so feeble about always wanting to be on good terms with people.

"No, no." Andy shook his head violently. "Truly it wasn't. At least I've no suspicions of any of them. Neither had she."

"But she did suspect somebody. And that day when you drove her to Swanhurst and she was so frustrated and worried when you drove her home— she'd been thinking of doing something about those suspicions, hadn't she, and then it all went wrong?"

Andy agreed that this was what he believed. "But I don't know who she suspected, truly I don't," he went on. "I wondered perhaps if it could have been her nephew. She did say he was a terrible driver and wouldn't care who he ran over as long as he got ahead."

"But did she have any definite evidence against him?"

"Only that he'd actually been to see her on the afternoon when it happened and could have been driving back to Swanhurst along Stubbs Lane. On the other hand he might have driven away in the other direction, since he'd said something about going on down to the coast, so she didn't know one way or the other."

Andy was frowning in the effort to remember everything. I was convinced that he was telling me all he knew, and his memory was exceedingly good. But oh, how I wished that I could have spoken to Miranda herself! Or that she had thought to approach me with her suspicions.

But perhaps she had intended to. I had been away having flu at the time she had come to see Geoff. But if she had wanted to see me personally, why hadn't she waited until I was back? Probably there was no simple answer. When one is irresolute about taking any action, as Miranda Porlock must have been about communicating her suspicions to a solicitor, then one is easily diverted from the purpose when things do not run smoothly.

Perhaps she had simply wanted to say to her conscience, "Well, I did try to do something, it wasn't my fault that I didn't get very far with it."

Andy was talking again, saying something along the lines of my own thoughts.

"It worried her all the time but she didn't know what to do for the best. There was this other possibility, you see."

Another possibility? Just when I was beginning to think that I should get no more information from the Country Cabs driver.

CHAPTER 7

He needed coaxing to tell me.

I had to swear to him and even offer to draft a document and sign it, that I would take no action against anybody as a result of anything he was going to say. I noted that he had not shown such qualms with regard to Mervyn. It seemed that nobody loved Mervyn, and I could almost begin to feel a faint twinge of pity for the man with the profile.

After all this buildup, I was expecting something more startling and more convincing than the next part of Andy's story. It concerned some unknown taxi-driver, which was no doubt why he had been so hesitant to tell me. On one occasion—several weeks before the date of Miranda's visit to Geoff—Andy had not been available when she asked for him, and she was told that none of the other drivers would be free immediately and that she would have to wait for half an hour. Apparently she had wanted a car rather urgently and had told them that for once she would use another firm.

When Andy next saw her, she told him about it. She had had an advertising circular come through the mail, she said, with the phone number of a new car-hire and taxi service and she thought she might as well try it. She had not been very impressed with the man who answered the phone: He sounded offhand and not particularly anxious for custom, but he had promised to send a car out to Mill Green straight away, and it did in fact turn up very quickly. She had not been impressed with the car, either. There was a noticeable dent in the side, and she told Andy she'd wondered if the brakes were all right.

But she had been very taken with the driver. A good-looking young man, obviously well educated, who told her he was a student doing this as a vacation job. His subject was philosophy and they had quite an interesting talk on the way to Swanhurst. She told him the shops she wanted to go to, and he seemed to know the town all right, and that was why she was surprised when he didn't take the turning down Stubbs Lane, which was the obvious way in to the centre of Swanhurst and all the other drivers always used it, but went the long way round instead. She asked him why he had done this, and he said he had forgotten about that short cut, but it struck her as odd and she had pursued the subject, and had actually mentioned that a woman had been killed in the lane by a hit-and-run driver some months earlier.

Andy could not—or would not—tell me the name of the firm that had sent the circular to Miss Porlock. She had not told him, he insisted; she had only said she would never use that firm again. Andy believed that she suspected the young driver of knowing something about the accident.

When he had finished his story, he asked me rather anxiously what I proposed to do.

"I shall probably make some attempt to trace that

driver," I replied, "but if it really was a student doing casual work it may not be easy. They come and go so much. And the firm itself sounds rather a fly-by-night affair. The ones who send out the glossiest circulars so often are. But whatever happens, I'll keep my promise. This is not going to lead to a prosecution. And in any case, I've got another line of enquiry to follow up first."

After Andy had gone, I sat for some time thinking over what he had said. His story was tantalising in that it seemed to bring me to the brink of a discovery, but only to the brink. I felt that I now had a much clearer picture of Miranda Porlock, and her great interest in Imogen's death would seem to bear out my own strong impression that she had made me her heir as a sort of gesture of compensation. But she had left it till almost too late, so whatever it was that her nephew had done finally to forfeit her trust must have been done near the end of Miranda's life, after she had been taken to hospital; in which case, that old evening paper I had still not had a chance to look at would be the only clue, and probably a very far-fetched one.

Unless she had heard something about Mervyn, on the very morning of the day she collapsed, that had caused her to come into Swanhurst. To do what? Come to our office to alter her will? Go to the police station to tell them of something he had done?

Whatever it was, it had caused her great uncertainty of mind, and she had asked Andy to leave her at the public gardens, where she would sit or walk and try to come to a decision. And while trying to do so, perhaps because of the strain and worry of doing so, and because she was already a very sick woman, she had suffered a severe heart attack, and an old man sitting on a bench nearby had seen her and had summoned an ambulance.

And that was the end of Miranda Porlock, apart from those few hours a week later when she rallied enough to dictate and sign that extraordinary will. It was no use wishing she had recovered enough to tell me her own tale. Unless I were to find some diaries or personal letters, which seemed very unlikely from what I knew of her, I was going to have to rely on other people to tell me what had been in Miranda's mind.

Other people. Not very many of them, and in most cases not very reliable witnesses. Not like the young taxi-driver. There was the "Rosemary" of the telephone-number list, who was to have some of Miranda's jewellery. She would know something, but I had the feeling that it was likely to be more about Miranda's distant past than about Miranda's recent life. Then, there were the hospital people, who were doing their best but knew so little; the people in the village of Mill Green—not very hopeful, but I had not yet exhausted that possibility; her nephew, who was hardly likely to co-operate with me in this respect or in any other; and lastly, my own partner, Geoffrey Holdsworth, whom I would have to tackle on the subject, because if Andy was to be believed, and I felt sure he was, then it looked as if Geoff had not told me the truth about his talk with Miranda Porlock.

I did not look forward to challenging him. In fact I didn't feel fit for it. My head was aching badly again after all the efforts and excitements of the morning. I had to see Miss Porlock's bank manager at half past two; there was a certain amount of routine correspondence to attend to; and I wanted to take time over my shopping for the dinner with Grace. This was quite a heavy enough programme for a semi-convalescent, and I decided to leave further investigations until tomorrow. By that time, I would have had the chance to discuss it all with Grace and would have slept on it.

So I went for a little stroll, had a sandwich and a drink, and then called at Miranda's bank, where the manager told me that he had always found her a businesslike person to deal with, but very reserved. It was almost a relief to me to find that he knew hardly anything about her apart from her financial situation. I felt that I had had enough revelations to be going on with, and could not cope with any more just yet. I was, however, interested to hear his views on Mervyn Porlock, whom he seemed to know more about than he did about his own client, Mervyn's aunt. He mentioned a case of art forgery that had been in and out of the papers in recent months, and said that Porlock had been suspected of being connected with it; he couldn't tell me any details, but he gave me the name and address of his informant, an acquaintance who was more knowledgeable about the art world than either of us were, and he told me to mention his name if I wished to get in touch with the man.

I thanked him and said I might well make use of this contact if Mervyn persisted in his attempts to upset his aunt's last will, and the bank manager was inclined to think that it was a lot of bluster and bluff; that Mervyn would give up, rather than face a lengthy lawsuit. I was not so sure; it would be wise not to take anything for granted where Mervyn Porlock was concerned. But then, I had the advantage of knowing just how unscrupulous he could be; my sore head was proof of it.

The rest of the day went according to plan, and by the time Grace arrived, the cheese was just turning brown on top of the fish-and-cream mixture and all preparations had been made for the meal. We ate and drank and talked about food and music and medicine and law, and it was so easy and comfortable that I was wishing we could go on like this the whole evening, and perhaps ever afterwards, just getting to know each other and feeling the joy of companionship, and forgetting about the whole business of Miranda Porlock, when Grace saved me from this temptation by introducing the subject herself.

"And now to business," she said as she took her coffee cup. "Come on, Harry. I know you're dying to report on your investigations. Here's your Dr. Watson, all ready to listen and admire."

"As a matter of fact I was just thinking I'd like to show you Imogen's cello before I finally bring myself to part with it."

"I'd love to see it, but let's leave it till next time. You'll never get rid of me now that I've discovered what a super cook you are; I shall insist on being invited again."

I made a little bow of acknowledgement and then said: "Wouldn't you rather tell me your life story?

I'd love to hear it. And in any case it's your turn now."

Her smile faded and she shook her head. "Later. I promise. Let's dispose of the Porlocks first."

With an effort, I set myself to the task of summarising my recent activities in connection with Miranda Porlock's estate. When I had finished my narration, Grace said: "You've definitely recovered, Harry, to be able to tell the whole story with as little emotion as if it were a clinical case history."

It pleased me so much to be told that I was unemotional, because usually I am accused of being the opposite, that of course I had instantly to contradict her.

"But I haven't been feeling coldly clinical at all! I've been back and forth like a swingometer. Falling in love with a house and wanting to murder Mervyn and disposing of thousands of pounds I haven't yet proved I possess to unknown young people—does that sound like a troubled mind regaining its balance?"

She just laughed.

"If I go on like this I'm going to be in trouble for unprofessional behaviour," I said.

She laughed again. "If they do disbar you, or whatever it is they do to solicitors, then you're free of the office for ever after and you can lie in the garden at Beth's Cottage listening to the bird song all day long. Mervyn's photograph," she added, suddenly sobering up. "That's very odd indeed."

"You don't believe he picked it up more or less on impulse after he'd got what he really wanted?"

"No, I don't. A big studio portrait is quite a bulky

thing, not like a ring or a necklace that you slip into your pocket. It's not the sort of thing you pick up as an afterthought when you're in a great hurry to get away. And he must have been in a great hurry. After all, Harry, you could have come round at any moment, and if you'd actually seen him. . . ."

"I agree that one would not waste time on inessentials in such circumstances."

"Not on inessentials, no. But supposing—"

"—that it was the photograph itself he was after!" I exclaimed.

We stared at each other for a moment, speechlessly.

"I thought of it, Grace," I said, "but it seemed quite absurd."

"Unless. . . ."

We said this together, our two minds racing for the same goal.

"Let's look at that paper," said Grace.

I pulled my chair round to the other side of the coffee-table and we spread out the old copy of the *Evening Gazette* and peered over it. What among all those pages of print would have made Miranda Porlock so agitated when she read it?

The air crash dominated the paper. Even the local news pages were full of a Sussex girl who had been killed in it; her photograph, and the long interview with the bereaved parents, covered many columns. Apart from that there were a suicide and a burglary and a stray-dog picture and story. Then came two pages of letters to the editor, mostly so idiotic or so unbelievably prejudiced that it made one despair for democracy and pray that one would never have to face a jury of one's fellow citizens. I said this to Grace and she said: "Yes, I know. Aren't we awful snobs?"

"We are indeed awful snobs. It's all right so long as there are a lot of us. It would be no fun being a snob all on one's own, because there would be nobody else to recognise how very superior one was. Here—don't turn the page yet. What's this down here?"

It was a short paragraph tucked away at the bottom of a column of advertisements and I had missed it on my first, quick reading, before Grace arrived. It was headed ART FORGERIES CLUE and stated that the police believed they were now on the track of the people who were master-minding the theft and forgery racket that had been going on for some months. A number of small drawings and sketches by famous artists, sold by reputable galleries, had turned out to be very clever copies of the originals, and some of the originals had actually come to light in the United States. It was not the gallery owners, but some of their customers, who had come under suspicion, the substitution being effected after the gallery had sold the drawing. Which meant that whoever bought it had then sold it twice over: the copy to a comparatively undiscriminating purchaser in Britain, and the original to a wealthy and unscrupulous collector overseas, who would not care about the forgery even if he knew of it.

Grace and I looked at each other and said with one voice: "Mervyn Porlock."

We returned to the newspaper. The clue, apparently, concerned the identity of the person who was actually making the copies of the drawings and who would, it was hoped, reveal the names of those for whom he was working.

That was all. The paper was now three days old. Neither of us had read or heard of any further developments since then, but presumably the enquiries were going on all the time and might soon bear fruit.

"Miranda had been suspecting him," I began.

"And reading this somehow confirmed her suspicions," said Grace.

"But she still couldn't bring herself openly to denounce her brother's son."

"So she cut him out of her will and left it all to you instead."

"It could make sense," I said slowly. "And the photograph—"

"—must have been what he wanted to get back immediately, because—"

"—the police were after one of the forgeries that he had in his possession—"

"—and he'd hidden it in the back of the frame and posted it to his aunt as a gift, knowing she wouldn't pull it to pieces, nor be at all interested in it, and that it would therefore be safe there—"

"—until he could collect it, but then he heard of her death—"

"—and that she'd left him nothing."

"And so—"

"—he had to retrieve it before some meddlesome solicitor found it and exposed the whole fraud."

We finished up together.

"And now what?" asked Grace.

"I tell the whole thing to this friend of Miranda's

bank manager, who knows all about the art world, and let him deal with it. I'm quite happy to make my statement and give evidence if it comes to court, but I don't want to take the initiative.

"If we're right about the photograph containing some sort of evidence against him, and about Miranda's motive for changing her will, then it looks as if that disposes of Mervyn," I said.

Grace agreed, and then we fell silent for a while. I felt that I ought to be pleased at the thought of disposing of Mervyn—in other words, of leaving him to the law to deal with if it did turn out that he was responsible for these frauds and cheats. It would save me the trouble of trying to find out any more about him, and he would surely be so busy defending himself and trying to keep out of jail that he would give up the fight over his aunt's will.

That would make things much easier all round. And yet even the prospect of inheriting Miranda's cottage did not save me from a sense of anticlimax, of vague disappointment. It was only a faint echo of the flatness I had felt earlier when I had swung violently round from believing that Mervyn had killed my wife into believing that he had had nothing to do with it, but nevertheless the disappointment was there, and Grace noticed it.

"You don't look very pleased at disposing of Mervyn," she said presently. "Were you looking forward to the contest over the will and getting your own back for your bump on the head?"

She spoke teasingly, but I had the impression that she, too, was in some way not quite contented, and this impression strengthened as we began to talk again.

"I don't want to fight him at all," I replied. "I don't like him and I'll be glad to be rid of him, but I feel cheated somehow, as if he's slipped out of my grasp. I mean, he was such a good candidate for the hit-and-run driver who killed Imogen, and now it looks as if we have to eliminate him."

"Because he also turns out to be a large-scale swindler? Are the two crimes mutually exclusive?"

There was a hint of her habitual irony in her voice, but I could sense tension in her as well.

"Not exactly," I replied, "but because of Miranda's attitude towards him. Andy Darren says, and I believe him, that Miranda always thought her nephew was not straight, and that she also thought it possible he might have run over my wife. But it must have been the first of these suspicions that mattered more to her, because it was what she saw as a confirmation of his crookedness that caused her to change her will. She didn't change her will because she thought he might have been the hit and run driver. Therefore she cannot have taken this possibility very seriously. On the other hand, Imogen's death was worrying her very much indeed, and she believed she might have a clue to it. But it wasn't Mervyn who was in her mind when she came to our office and saw Geoff. It must have been somebody else. Possibly this young temporary driver who didn't want to go down Stubbs Lane. Possibly some-one quite different, whom not even Andy knows about. But did she actually tell Geoff anything? That's what I want to know. And if she did—or even if she didn't, come to that—I want to know what really happened at that interview. Is Geoff deliberately telling me lies? Or has he got some daft idea of not wanting to upset me by going over Imogen's death all over again?"

Grace replied to my rhetorical questions by asking some other questions and demanding answers to them. "It looks as if you might have reached a critical point in your hunt for the truth. Harry, are you quite sure you really want to find out what really happened? And did you really mean it when you told Andy that if you did discover who was driving that car, you would take no action against the driver and you would not make it public in any way?"

She turned in her chair to look straight at me as she spoke, and I had the impression that she was under considerable strain.

"You're afraid that I might not like what I find out," I said. "I've been afraid of it too, Grace. Sometimes I thought it was somebody near to me who killed Imogen, and that was a terrible thought, that I might actually be meeting and talking with the person who held this secret. And I dreaded knowing, because I felt I should kill them if I knew. I felt so violent for revenge. But it's all gone now. It's like recovering from an illness. It was Miranda Porlock who worked the miracle for me, and got rid of my dreadful sickness of vengeance. And you played a great part in it yourself, Grace."

She screwed up her face as I said these last words and made a little gesture as if pushing something away. Was she so afraid of any emotion that she could not even bear to be thanked? I wondered; or did she detect signs of instability in me that I, in my new-found hope and desire to live, was not conscious of, myself?

"Don't you believe me?" I asked. "Are you afraid that if it came to the test, I would, after all, find myself demanding retribution?"

She shook her head, looking more and more distressed.

"We'll have some music," I said. "We won't talk about it any more."

I shut my eyes as we listened to the Mozart *Requiem*. It was as if I was saying farewell to Imogen. I had never responded to the music in quite that way before. By the time the record came to an end, I had momentarily forgotten that I was not alone, and I believe I actually said aloud: "Now I must let her go."

Then I looked up at my visitor, hoping my words had not been heard.

Grace was leaning back in the armchair with her head resting against one of its wings and her hands covering her face. For a second or two I saw her as a brightly coloured portrait that could be given the title "Despair." There was the olive green of her dress against the yellow upholstery, and the hands looked pale against the red tints of her hair. Good, strong, capable hands. They didn't move. She is weeping and does not want it to be seen, I thought, and I picked up the tray with the coffee things and took it into the kitchen and occupied myself there for some minutes. Then I called out: "I'm making some tea for myself—what about you, Grace?"

"Some for me, please," she called back.

When I returned to the sitting-room she was studying the record sleeve of the Mozart record and looked quite calm and composed.

"Thanks, Harry," she said. "You are the soul of tact. I think Imogen was a very lucky woman."

"So she used to say. But I always felt that the greater luck was on my side."

"I wish I'd known her," said Grace.

She drank her tea, put the cup back on the table, and said in a voice of false brightness: "Now you're in for it, Harry. I'm going to tell you a revoltingly corny sob story. God, how I do loathe self-pity!" she cried loudly, sitting up straight and staring at me with fury in her eyes, challenging me to utter a word of sympathy, daring me to try to comfort her.

I stared back. I knew I should have to respond but that it was vitally important that I say the right thing. One false step now and she would clam right up again and something of very great value would be lost for ever. It was a moment of almost agonising suspense. I felt it first as music, as the sinister and ominous rhythm at the end of the third movement of the Beethoven Fifth Symphony. And then it seemed to me as if Grace and I were in a small boat on the ocean, and far on the horizon was a faint glow that brought the hope of land, and I held the power to bring us safely there if I could but discover the right way to use it.

I must say the right thing, and it was doubly difficult because I myself was so deeply involved. I was in a state of excitement mixed with incredulity that was almost physically painful. Why should I,

Harry Johnson, be so much favoured by the gods? For it looked as if Fate, that had snatched from me one jewel, was now offering me another, very different in kind, but of the greatest worth. I was overwhelmed, almost stifled by the sense of hope and promise. But this gift would not come easily: I should have to fight for it with every bit of my heart and mind.

Oh, Imogen, please help me, I cried out in my thoughts; please tell me what to say. The words came, it seemed from outside myself, just as they had come when I stood on the spot where Imogen had died and a voice had told me that I should find the truth and the truth would set me free. I spoke them aloud, very calmly, very steadily.

"I hate self-pity too. And I hate to be pitied by others. But a lot of that is due to pride. And pride is no virtue, it's a vice. The saddest and the loneliest of all the seven deadly sins."

I heard her give a little gasp and I looked away, convinced that I had failed and that though we might continue for some while to sail on that ocean in some sort of friendship, we should never reach that land. Then she spoke again, in her usual restrained manner, and I knew that all was well and felt weak with relief.

"You are quite right," she said. "I am very guilty of the sin of pride. I always have been. The strange thing is that nobody, not even those very near and dear to me, has ever had the courage to say so to my face."

"Fools rush in where angels fear to tread." It

didn't matter what I said now. She wouldn't shut herself away again. At any rate, not from me.

"Don't fish for compliments," said Grace. "You're not getting any more now. You're going to get my life story, God help you."

CHAPTER 8

"You'll have guessed by now that I am a mourner too," said Grace.

"Yes," I replied. "We seem to recognise each other instinctively, we the bereaved."

"I was born and brought up in Sydney. My grandparents emigrated from Scotland and started a business which turned out very successfully. Garages and car hire." She smiled faintly. "A rather larger concern than your Country Cabs. My parents inherited a lot of money and I was reared quite in luxury. I'm an only child. In fact I was very spoilt, and when I decided I wanted to be a doctor and do my training at a Scottish university, they let me have that, too.

"I've worked here ever since. I visit my parents often, but I've never wanted to live in Australia again. Besides, up till about nine months ago I had my daughter to think of. Adela. She was just nineteen. She was illegitimate. She was a drug addict. She killed herself."

Grace brought out these short sentences with a quick, angry, aggressive manner, as if she were making stabs at herself.

"Yes," I said, "I remember the other night, when

we were talking about bereavement, you said that loss by suicide was the worst of all."

She looked a little better now that she had spoken and I had answered very calmly. She even made an effort to smile and speak in her usual, detached voice. "There's a sort of rivalry in misfortune, isn't there? If you've got to go through with this sort of thing, I suppose it helps a bit to feel you've had as bad as can be. Sort of claiming a position at the top of the hierarchy."

"I don't think it makes any difference," I said, speaking much more warmly than I had before. "You also said that evening that one can't compare different sorts of misery, and I agree with that."

"Did I say that?" The mask had slipped again and she looked haggard and old.

I nodded. I was aching to burst out into a flood of sympathy but knew that I must not do so. My task was to control myself and listen to her as quietly and calmly as she had listened to me.

"It's rather difficult," she said. "I've never talked about it to anyone before. I mean, I've had to talk about it, of course, but I've always adjusted the story to suit the feelings or expectations of the person I was telling it to."

This time I could not contain myself. "Oh, I know, I know!" I cried. "That's what one does. It's a sort of easy way out. It's as if other people's expectations sort of hold you together. Like air pressure."

"So what do you expect me to do now, Harry?"

"Well, to start with you could have a pretty good howl. As I did."

She actually laughed. "I thought I was going to,

but it seems to have passed off. If you can bear it, I think I'll just talk. It's getting very late, though."

"Eleven o'clock. Do the medical staff get a reprimand if they're not in by midnight on their days off?"

"I'm not on call till nine tomorrow morning, but what about you and your sore head?"

"Now you're just making excuses. Come on, Grace. You heard all my drama. Let me hear yours. No? All right. Let me guess it. Correct me when I go wrong. Young Grace Watson arrives from Australia—very clever and determined and devoted to her career but maybe having led a somewhat sheltered life?"

She nodded.

"So it's all very exciting, this new world of learning and practising and meeting people with similar tastes and interests and ambitions. Very different to what it was back home. She's made of sterling stuff, this Grace, so she doesn't lose her head and ruin her career, but she does go and fall in love. Not a fellow student, I think. Too immature. One of her teachers. Married."

"Right first time," said Grace.

"The child was not intended, but she really does want it to be born."

"Right again."

"So she struggles along somehow, bringing up her daughter and carrying on with her medical career, working round the clock—"

"No, Harry, you're going wrong now," Grace interrupted me. "Adela wasn't born until after I'd qualified and I didn't suffer any physical hardships.

My parents were actually thrilled to have a grand-daughter, even an illegitimate one. In a way, being at such a distance made it easier for them, but they came over and looked after me and bought me a house and helped financially. So it isn't the usual grim tale of survival. And Adela's father helped too, and took a lot of interest in her."

"But no question of sorting it all out?"

"Oh, no. He is—or was; he's dead now—an impossible person to live with. Brilliant as a surgeon, hopeless in everyday life. I would never have married him, nor he me. His wife acted hostess for him when necessary, but otherwise they went their separate ways. It suited all three of us to leave things as they were. Don't you believe me? Don't you believe people can love each other but genuinely not want to live with each other all the time?"

"I believe you," I replied. "I know it's possible. But I happen to have been exceptionally lucky, myself. I've always realised that. What went wrong, then, Grace?"

"Adela. I ought never to have allowed her to be born. As she was so fond of telling me."

She spoke with a bitterness that I had never heard in her before. I remained silent. She didn't need much prompting now.

"Adela was healthy, tough, intelligent. And since she had more of her father's looks than of mine, she was handsome, too. She was much loved. We had many friends. She did well at school but liked to torment me by saying she didn't think she'd trouble to take any exams. I'd have liked her to do justice to her gifts, but I don't think I pressed her too hard.

Neither in that nor in other ways. Perhaps that was the trouble. Perhaps I didn't demand enough."

Grace was leaning forward now with her hands clasped lightly together, staring at the gas fire and talking in a low but steady voice.

"Maybe if she had suffered more frustration and unhappiness it would not all have become concentrated on the fact that her parents were not married to each other. She needed a grievance. I don't believe it would have been any better if Gregory and I had married. She'd have found other reasons why she was the most ill-used and unjustly treated creature that ever was. A life of real hardship and privation. That might have kept her alive. Always the victim. Oh, the self-torture of it!" Grace gave a little shudder. "Where did she get it from? Greg was unstable in many ways, but not in that way. And I myself—do I strike you as a psychiatric case, Harry?"

"No indeed. Very much the opposite."

"But no psychiatrist could help my poor Adela. It was as if she had been programmed to live and die the way she did. I suppose in a way she was right. If it had to be like that, then it would have been better if she had never been born. But how was I to know that it had to be like that? How could I have stopped it?"

"You couldn't have known and you couldn't stop it. But you still blame yourself."

"I used to, but not so much now. My reason tells me I am not to blame. But my reason has to fight very hard to keep me steady. Very hard indeed."

"How did she die? Would you like to tell me?"

"Exactly as she had lived. A self-torturing victim.

For several years she had lived with other drug takers like herself, coming home for a few days now and then to be nursed and to make scenes about how I had ruined her life. I'd moved to London by then and was doing locum jobs so that I'd be free to give all my attention to Adela if she needed me. Much of the time I had no idea where she was. The last time I saw her was about three months before I heard of her death. She rang the bell at three in the morning and I thought she wouldn't live till dawn. God knows what she'd been pouring into herself beside the heroin. She pulled through once again, though, and I expected the usual abuse as soon as she was feeling better, but this time it didn't come. The depression seemed to have gone too deep. Instead of blaming me, she blamed herself. And do you know, Harry? That was almost worse. In fact it was much worse."

Grace glanced at me and then quickly looked back at the fire again.

"Much worse. It was as if the blaming me had been some sort of defence, and now all the defences were gone. I tried yet again to get her into treatment, but she disappeared as soon as she was on her feet again and I never heard from her any more. Not until the police told me she had been found dead, abandoned by her companions in a house where they had been squatting. That was her end. Alone. She had left even the refuge for addicts where she had had some attention and care, and had joined this group of strangers. Overdose of drink and drugs was the verdict, but of course the truth was that she had killed herself. It was no accident. She had slowly but surely been killing herself for years. Perhaps all her life."

"And you?"

"I thought of going back to Australia to try to comfort my parents. They were heart-broken about Adela's life and death. But I didn't feel I could face it immediately. Neither did I feel able to face any of my friends. Work seemed the best answer. I'd been here for some while as a locum and they offered me a permanency, so I took it."

She leaned back and shut her eyes and looked utterly exhausted.

I no longer felt the great upsurge of sympathy that dared not speak itself. I felt nothing. What does one say to a story like this? There is nothing to say. And yet speak one must.

"Did you find that Miranda Porlock's death helped you in some strange way?" I asked.

It was not what I had intended to say: It just slipped out, as these things sometimes do.

Grace opened her eyes. "Yes. It did help. But it frightened me too."

"Frightened you? Why?"

"Because I had the feeling something was being let loose and could run out of control."

I begged her to be more specific. She could only repeat that she had this generalised but very strong sense of apprehension.

"Was that why you warned me that I might be disappointed if I ever found out the truth about Imogen's death?" I asked.

"I suppose so." She looked puzzled and worried and dissatisfied. "I don't know why I've got this sense of doom. Normally I am all for the truth at all costs. Except for sick people who can't stand it; but that's different. Or perhaps it isn't. I think it's something to do with the fact that I believe Adela had at last recognised the truth about herself and that was what finally destroyed her."

She stood up, yawning and rubbing her eyes.

"Harry, I'll have to go. You'd think unburdening yourself would make you refreshed, but it seems to have worn me out. Thank you for everything. And good luck. Don't take any notice of my fears. It's probably just that I'm still trying to come to terms with things, myself."

"When do we meet again?" I asked at the front door. "And where?"

"Could I come and see this house you've fallen in love with?"

We fixed to spend the day together on Sunday, two days later, and I would call for her at the hospital.

"And no more confessionals and life histories," added Grace. "We're going to have a happy day."

"Music and Beth's Cottage and talk. We're going to have a happy day," I repeated.

But at the door of her car she suddenly caught hold of me and we clung together. Her sense of apprehension communicated itself to me, and I was once again struggling in the waters of the ocean. It was as if our little boat was going to sink, right now, within sight of land.

"It's all right, Grace," I said, comforting her at last. "Your doom thing is just the reaction from giving way at last after holding it all in for so long. It will pass, truly it will."

"It will pass," she agreed. "Thank you again. Sleep well."

But I did not sleep well that night. Grace's story had disturbed me very deeply; my mind was racing with my own discoveries of the day, and I was very anxious about the heart to heart talk that I was determined to have with Geoff. Grace's words kept going through my head: "Harry, are you quite sure you really want to find out what happened?"

Had she guessed something? Did she have some gift of prophecy? Or was it simply, as we had both tried to convince ourselves it was, a vague sense of apprehension arising from tiredness and strain?

"Tell me, Imogen," I said, switching on the light and looking at her photograph on my bedside table, "what you would like me to do."

The candid face stared back at me. She seemed very far away. And yet so near that there was no separating myself from her.

"I have to know the truth in order to be free," I said almost defensively. "That's what my inner voice told me. But Grace has made me doubt. You would like Grace, Imogen. She is wise and good. And strong but very vulnerable. If ever she agrees to take your place I shall need to save her from hurt. Just as I believe she is trying to save me. She fears I could hurt both myself and others by stirring up the past. She could well be right. I know I am not going to seek punishment for your killer, but does your killer know that? I might endanger myself and others. I might ruin lives. Oh, Imogen, what shall I do?"

When day came, I realised that I had no choice.
I'd already gone too far to turn back. Truth is indi-
visible. Like peace. You cannot take out the bits you
want and leave the rest.

At least there was one matter about which I had
no doubt. I rang the number that Miranda's bank
manager had given me and drove down to a village
near Brighton to see a retired art historian who had
made the criminal side of the world of art dealing
his special hobby. We took to each other at once and
he had many a fascinating story to tell.

"Porlock's a stupid fellow," he said. "If he'd been
content with two or three successes and then left
that type of forgery alone and turned to a different
sort of trick, instead of pushing his luck too far—but
then, they always think they can get away with it for
ever."

"And there's the blackmail angle too," I said. "If
this man Carter could forge drawings but not paint-
ings, he'd be pressing to keep on with the racket.
And Porlock would be at his mercy. I'm almost beginning to feel sorry for him."

We talked for a couple of hours and agreed to
keep in touch. I told him briefly about my own in-
volvement with the Porlocks but said nothing about
my search for the driver who killed my wife. It was a
pleasure to forget about it for a while, and I drove
back to Swanhurst feeling refreshed and more ready
for the talk with my partner.

Geoff had been out all morning too, attending to
his son's defence on the drugs charge. Bail had been
allowed and the case was to be heard in three weeks'
time. Meanwhile Peter had agreed to remain at

home, much to his father's relief but not so much to
his mother's.

Sheila Holdsworth was a handsome, well-pre-
served woman who was a leading light in Swanhurst society. Her manners were perfect and her
house was perfect and she was the perfect hostess.
Appearances again. That was what mattered to
Geoff, and he had got it. She always treated me very
correctly, but I could not get to like her, because I
felt it was impossible to get to know her. She and
Imogen had nothing in common, and our occasional
foursomes had been stilted. Maybe underneath the
shiny exterior Sheila was a nervous and insecure person. Maybe she really was a cold and unfeeling person. I didn't know. I only knew that Geoff took his
cue from her in all things, that he was longing for
me to be out of the office for good, and that he cared
more deeply for Peter than Sheila did.

Poor Pete. He had either to shine in the way his
parents wanted or else gain attention by becoming a
nuisance. Since he had only average ability, he could
not follow the first course, so he had to choose the
latter.

"Peter has always had a great respect for you,
Harry," Geoff was saying. "If you've got time, I wonder if you'd mind inviting him round and talking to
him a bit."

"Of course," I replied. "I'll be glad to see him if
he'd like to come."

I didn't believe in the "great respect," but I could
quite see that Geoff would be glad to get Peter out of
the house as much as possible.

But the talk with my partner was going very badly

for my own purposes. I was feeling more and more sympathetic towards him every minute, and less and less in the mood for accusing him of lying to me about Miranda Porlock. I ought to have made a surprise attack on him then, when he was at his most vulnerable, unhappy about his son and depending on me for comfort. That would have broken him down. But I could not do it.

We were sitting upstairs in his room, and Jenny rang through to say that a client had arrived for his appointment with Mr. Holdsworth. My opportunity was gone, and yet I could not bear to leave the room without having said something. I had screwed myself up to it and could not endure the thought of doing so all over again on a future occasion.

"Oh, by the way, Geoff," I said as I got up from my chair, "can you remember whether Miss Porlock mentioned her nephew at all that time she came to see you at the office?"

A feeble little shot, giving him every chance to prevaricate. He opened the file of the client he was about to see and studied it for a moment without replying. Then he said: "Sorry, Harry, I wasn't listening. I've got quite a problem here. What did you say?"

I repeated my question. He frowned and seemed to be thinking hard.

"She might have mentioned him in passing. He wasn't much help to her. Poor old lady all alone. That sort of thing. Why? Are you having trouble with him?"

"Not particularly. It looks as if he could be. in-

volved in a case of art forgery and I doubt whether
he'll be putting up much of a fight over her will."

"Art forgery?"

I explained very briefly. Geoff knew about the
case but hadn't known that Mervyn was under suspicion.

"If they're wanting any evidence from me, I'm
afraid I can't help," he said. "I'm quite sure his aunt
didn't refer to this at all when she came to see me."

I was watching him closely. He looked and
sounded very relieved. So I have at least learnt
something, I thought as I left the room. Whatever it
was that Miranda talked to him about, it certainly
was not her nephew and his misdeeds; it was something much closer to Geoffrey's heart.

Close to his heart.

I was half-way down the stairs, staring at the fanlight over the front door, when it suddenly hit me
like lightning and I stood still. Why hadn't I seen it
before? Because my mind was so set on Mervyn, because I could not endure the thought that the driver
who ran over my wife could be someone well known
to me? Oh, Grace, how right you were! How wise
you are! All my brave words about facing the truth;
they faded to nothing now that I actually saw in my
mind's eye the face of Imogen's killer.

My heart was racing. I hung on to the banisters
and stared at the tracery of the fanlight and could
not move.

"Excuse me."

I was blocking the way of Geoffrey's client, an elderly man with a limp. I moved aside to let him pass,
and walked slowly down to my room. Marilyn came

in with a message for me, interrupted herself before she had finished giving it.

"Mr. Johnson! Are you all right? Is it your head again?"

I said I'd been up too late the night before, and got rid of her by asking if she would bring me some black coffee. Then I sat down at my desk and looked out at the familiar view of the patch of grass and the laburnum tree and recovered my balance.

Peter Holdsworth. The black sheep of the family. The weak boy with a charming manner if he chose to assume it. The light and the despair of his father's life. Always in trouble. Squatting. Drugs. And driving while disqualified. This last had been eighteen months ago, before Imogen's death. He'd got off lightly; he'd do it again. And yet again.

My thoughts raced.

I'd say no more to Geoff. Let's keep things calm between us. Geoff was going to need my help. If he'd accept it when he knew that I knew. Had he known all along? I hoped not, for both our sakes. I hoped he had not known till Miranda told him her suspicions. That would make things easier for us both. Poor Geoff.

And poor Pete.

Ah, thank God, thank God. I shut my eyes and rested my head on my hand and felt a great wave of relief. It was too good to last. The fury would come flooding back, would ebb and flow for some time to come. But it would go in time, because just for a second I had felt a stab of genuine pity for the boy who had killed my wife.

Marilyn came in with the coffee and I told her I was feeling better. She wanted to know how I had got on with the art expert. With a great effort, I turned my mind to the events of the morning. They seemed light-years away.

"He knew quite a bit about your bête noire," I said.

"Mervyn Porlock?"

We talked about the case. I was beginning to feel almost grateful to Mervyn. His misdeeds were enabling me to avoid all sorts of awkward conversations. Marilyn knew Peter Holdsworth, had actually been rather taken with him at one time. No doubt his latest exploit was already all round the office, but I didn't want to talk to anyone about it. I wanted to talk to Peter as soon as I felt calm enough, but would Peter want to talk to me?

Well, he had simply got to keep in with his father at the moment, and if his father pressed him—

Suddenly it struck me as rather odd that Geoff should be urging me to be a friend to Peter if he knew that Peter had killed my wife. Could it be that I was wrong, after all, and that the flash of illumination was a mirage?

I went over all the factors that had led up to that revelation on the stairs and decided that I was not wrong in essentials. Whatever my partner knew or did not know, whatever complex of motives had led him to ask me to talk to his son, there was no doubt in my mind that in one way or another Peter Holdsworth was going to lead me to the heart of the mystery.

CHAPTER 9

He came round to my house about six o'clock that evening and I suggested that we drive out to Mill Green and I would show him the house I had inherited. It would be easier than sitting and talking in a room filled with the memory of Imogen.

On the way there I did not look at him. Best keep it cool for the time being. I asked whether he wanted to discuss the drugs charge and he said, not really, he was getting rather sick of it. I said I could understand that and wished him luck. Personally I had never felt strongly about cannabis, and this latest adventure of Pete's seemed to me about as harmless as anything he had ever been accused of, although—such are the oddities of the law—it could well be the one that finally landed him in jail.

"Anyway, I don't care one way or the other," he said.

We had stopped at traffic lights, and I glanced at the boy sitting by my side. He looked white and tired and very young. I drove on again, feeling something I had never experienced before: an extraordinary tenderness for the boy, combined with a wish that he was my own son, that I might have the right to care for him. I remained deep in these thoughts for the rest of the short drive through the spring countryside, and Peter said nothing more.

When I drew up on the patch of grass in front of Beth's Cottage I said: "Here we are. This is my surprise inheritance."

"Yes, I know," said Peter.

I felt a momentary surprise before I remembered that if my theory was correct, he had been here before. The tenderness remained, but agitation entered in. It didn't look as if he was going to make any pretence. But could I bear to hear his confession? I thought of Grace again and for a moment or two sincerely wished that I had never embarked on this search. Then I looked back at the deadness of the time since Imogen died and I knew there had been no choice. I was fighting for my own survival, like every other living thing.

"But did you actually go into the house when you fetched Miss Porlock to drive her to Swanhurst?" I asked as we went through the gate and walked along the path between the daffodils.

"No," said Pete.

"Then, come and look at it now. I think you'll like it. It's just as she left it."

I went ahead of him and thought: Well, here's his chance. If he wants to knock me on the head and make a better job of it than Mervyn did, he's got nobody to stop him, and nobody knows we're here. I asked myself the question: If I knew I was about to be murdered, would I really care? The answer came quickly: No, not really, provided it was quick and comparatively painless. But almost in the same second I thought: If I die now, I'll never see the apple

blossoms in the orchard here. And I'll never see
Grace again.

It was very strange. I cared and yet I did not care.
Everything in my world had become enormously
precious and yet I could endure to let it go. I wonder
if Imogen felt like this, I thought; were her last
thoughts of music or of me? Or of the dog, or of
nothing, before the final pain.

Peter was wandering about the long living-room.
"Yes, I like it," he said.

"What did you think of Miss Porlock herself?"

He had picked up a blue-and-white bowl from the
window sill at the far end of the room, where we
stood looking out at the orchard, and he turned it
over and over in his hands as he replied.

"I liked her. Even though—"

The bowl slipped through his fingers and broke
into fragments on the floor. It was only at this moment that I realised the full extent of his nervousness
under the dead-pan manner.

"Christ!" he cried. "I'm sorry. Was it valuable?"

His father speaking in him; was it valuable?

"I've no idea," I replied. "Does it matter? It
wasn't alive. It didn't hurt it to break."

He looked at me with a horrified expression on his
face, and then his features crumpled up and he sank
down on his knees by the sofa and banged his head
and his fists against the side of it like a child in a tan-
trum. I wandered off to the other end of the room
and yet again turned over the piles of receipts and
circulars that lay on top of the little rosewood desk.
After a while I heard Peter say, "Sorry about that,"
and I looked up to see that he was sitting on the

sofa, apparently in control of himself. I came across to him and perched myself on the arm and said nothing.

"I didn't kill her," he said.

Words rose to my lips: I'm not sure I believe you, but if you didn't, then I'm quite sure you know who did. I bit back the words and said nothing.

"Dad thinks I did," went on Peter.

It seemed safe enough then to ask, "Why?"

"Because of Miss Porlock. She told him she thought it was me, because of what we talked about that day."

The story came out quickly: There was no need for me to ask questions.

It had been last summer, during the long vacation. Peter was spending a few days at home. There were great arguments because he said he didn't want to go back to college in the autumn but was going to join a group going overland to India. The usual sort of thing. But he was short of money as usual and couldn't pay for his share of the expenses of the project. Naturally his parents wouldn't help. Where to find money? He knew a man who was trying to start up a taxi business and offered himself as a driver. It didn't trouble him that he'd been banned from driving for a year and the year was not yet up. Nor did it trouble the man in question.

"It was only a sideline," said Peter. "He was mostly dealing in used cars."

"I see," I said.

"I said I'd drive for him if he ever got any orders, and that's how I came to Miss Porlock. It was the first order he'd had, and after I told him about her he said he wouldn't take any more and if anyone else rang he'd say they'd gone out of business. She was inquisitive, you see."

"Yes," I said, remembering my talk with Andy Darren, of Country Cabs, "I gather that she liked to look into things."

"But I liked her, all the same. We talked about Kant and the nature of appearances when we were driving back, and that's when I told her my father was all for appearances and nothing else, and she was interested, and then everything sort of slipped out."

"Everything?"

"Well, not absolutely everything, but quite a lot of it. I told her about the situation at home and about my various troubles, and I admitted I ought not to be driving, because I had no licence. She wanted to know if this was the first time I'd driven since the conviction and I said, No, it wasn't, and then she told me to stop the car—we were about a mile away from here—and she began to cross-examine me. Dates, times, places. Why hadn't I come down Stubbs Lane on our way in to Swanhurst? All that sort of thing. Mixture of psychological and factual."

He stopped talking and it was all I could do to stop myself from questioning him and to wait in silence until he spoke again.

"It's funny," he said. "I ought to've been angry with Miss Porlock for telling my father all about it, but I wasn't. She said I ought to tell him myself, and I said I could not face it, and she said, then she would have to do it herself, but she didn't want to face it either."

"I gather she was very doubtful about doing so right up to the last moment," I commented. "It seems to have caused her a great deal of worry. You ought to have talked to him yourself, Peter."

"I know. And it would probably have been less harrowing in the end than it turned out to be after she'd seen him." He gave a little shudder. "I've never seen Dad like that."

"More in sorrow than in anger?"

Pete shook his head. "No. Nothing but anger. I thought he was going to have apoplexy. And he simply would not believe that I didn't kill—"

He broke off abruptly and I had to finish for him. "That you did not run over Imogen."

"He wouldn't believe it." Peter shook his head again and seemed unable to stop. It jerked from side to side for several seconds before he continued. "I did come home for a few days after the accident, and I simply could not prove that I was anywhere else when it actually happened. I'd been banned from driving for several weeks by then, but I had friends who let me drive their cars. I told my father this and I had an idiotic idea that if I told him truthfully about all the crimes I really had committed, then he'd be more likely to believe me when I said I hadn't committed that particular one. But it didn't work. Don't you believe me?"

He looked straight at me. A fair young man with grey-blue eyes and well-formed features. A weak and appealing young man. And a frightened one. What did he see me as? I wondered. A very average-looking elderly man; a tiresome old man no longer able to handle his job but refusing to give way to a younger partner? Someone he could talk to and trust? Or just as a man whose life he himself had shattered?

We stared at each other and I didn't know what to believe. In the end I said: "I don't know, Peter. I'd like to believe you. I think the odds are that you are speaking the truth. Probably nothing but the truth. But not the whole truth." I paused and then pounced. "But if you didn't kill my wife, then I am quite sure you know who did."

He shifted and blinked and we stared at each other again.

"All right," I said at last. "I believe it wasn't you. But I believe you know who it was."

He didn't contradict me.

"Was it your father?" I asked casually.

"Good God, no!" His amazement was genuine.

"Your mother?"

"Mother never puts a foot wrong," he said bitterly.

My opinion exactly, but on the other hand there is an exception to every rule. Sheila was as competent at driving as she was at everything else, but if she ever did slip up I had no doubt that she would not even stop at murder in order to convince everybody that it had not been her fault. I was thinking about Geoff's wife and trying to readjust my theories, which seemed to be for ever requiring readjustment, when Peter spoke of his own accord.

"It's no good asking me any more. It wasn't anybody you've ever met."

His tone was abrupt, almost aggressive, but it had the ring of truth.

Nobody I'd ever met. My last remaining theory collapsed in ruins, and I didn't know whether I was relieved or disappointed.

"And anyway they're dead now," Peter was saying, "so can't you leave it alone?"

Dead? My thoughts were reeling. Could it, after all, have been Miranda herself? But if so, why had she pursued Imogen's killer, even to the point of telling Geoff she believed it was his son? In theory one might say that Miranda's "investigations" were directed not towards finding the culprit but towards finding out whether anybody suspected her. But it didn't square with anything I knew of Miranda. Besides, Peter had said it was nobody I'd ever met, and I'd certainly met Miranda, and Peter knew it.

"If it was a friend of yours who is no longer alive, then I quite see there's no point enquiring any further, and I'm sorry you've been distressed over it," I said. "But, Peter—forgive me if I sound interfering— I can understand being loyal to the dead as well as to the living, but in fairness to yourself I do feel that your father should know."

"He wouldn't believe me. He'd think I was sheltering behind someone who could no longer speak for themselves."

"But surely— Well, anyway, I believe you."

"I know. But you're not my father."

"I wish I could help," I said.

"Help whom? Me or Dad?" He was bitter and desolate now.

"Help you, of course."

"It's too late. I'll soon be in prison."

"That's not certain yet. Would money help, Pete?"

"I'm not scrounging off you." Aggression once more.

"Of course not. But I have to distribute some of Miss Porlock's estate amongst needy people. I should think you'd qualify. Wait till the hearing is over and then let's talk again."

He looked as miserable as ever, but I had the feeling that I might have gained a little ground.

"Anyway," I went on, "I promise you that my investigation is at an end. If I'd known before that it was a friend of yours who ran over my wife, my enquiries would never have begun. Nor would Miss Porlock's. I don't think she would have accused you of sheltering behind the dead. Anyway, thanks for telling me. What would you like to do now? Join me for a meal somewhere?"

"I think I'd like to be alone for a bit. No offence. I'm just tired of talking."

"Don't blame you. We'll go back to Swanhurst and you tell me where you want to be put down."

Peter said nothing at all on the return drive; yet, after we had parted, I felt very lonely. It was not the aching blackness of mourning: It was just a grey emptiness. Any reasonably cheerful company would have eased it. I thought of my friends, those whom I had not succeeded in driving away completely during the months when I had been inconsolable and intolerable, and I made a few telephone calls and fixed a few engagements and felt a little better. Then I began to plan what I would do with Miranda's estate, and to dream of making her house into my home, and that helped too.

But the greatest comfort of all was the knowledge that I was to see Grace again on Sunday. I would tell her that she was to have her wish: My search for the truth was now at an end.

And no harm done. Well, not very much. At any rate, not to anybody now alive. Imogen was dead and so was the young man who had killed her. Presumably he had been drunk, probably driving without a licence. Just as Peter himself had been when he was had up for dangerous driving.

But Peter had been lucky in his wildness. His victims had been a parked car and a woman with minor cuts and bruises. It could have been very different. His own fate might very easily have been that of his friend. No wonder he was so reluctant to give the name, so willing to let himself be unjustly accused. I had a mental image of a young man not unlike Peter. He was dead now. How had he died? Killed himself in yet another piece of crazy driving?

Peter would probably tell me about it sooner or later. I felt mildly curious, but no longer desperate to know. The talk with Geoffrey's son was the climax of my search; the driving force behind that search was almost spent. As I ate my meal, I went over it all in my mind, sorting out the details before closing the file, and that was how I came to remember that I had not yet tried to get in touch with the "Rosemary" whose telephone number was among the few that Miranda Porlock had noted for use, and who, according to the scribbled memo, was to have some of Miranda's jewellery.

I felt a great reluctance to make this call. I feared more revelations, and I was sick of revelations. Let Imogen rest, let my revenge die its natural death, and let me slowly learn how to fill the emptiness of life again. Grace had given me a glimpse of the way; with her help, I should learn my lesson.

Of course I had to dial the number in the end. It was part of my duty as executor. A woman's voice answered.

"I'm sorry to trouble you, but are you the 'Rosemary' who is acquainted with Miss Miranda Porlock, of Mill Green?" I asked carefully.

The voice admitted that it was. Mrs. Rosemary Corbett.

I quickly explained the situation. She had not known that Miranda was dead, and I gave her the particulars of the funeral and explained about the memo with her name. We talked for some time. I need not have feared revelations. Rosemary Corbett was a friend of Miranda's childhood. They spoke on the telephone perhaps two or three times a year. They had not met for at least three years. The sketch that the young taxi-driver had given me of Miranda was filled in considerably. Mrs. Corbett sounded a pleasant, sensible sort of person, concerned about Miranda but resigned to letting her go her own way. I asked her when they had last talked, and she said about ten days before. The evening before Miranda was taken to hospital.

"We talked about her health," said Mrs. Corbett. "She hardly ever mentioned it, but this time she said she must tell somebody. She believed she was very ill, but she couldn't bear the thought of being kept alive against her will. Then we talked about her nephew, as we usually did. I couldn't decide anything for her. I could only listen. I had the impression she had definitely made up her mind to disinherit him. She asked me what she should do with her money then, and I begged her not to leave it to me! I'm getting old and I've got plenty to live on, and I don't want to be bothered with lawyers."

I laughed and she said: "Well, you know what I mean, Mr. Johnson. Nothing personal. Anyway, I said surely she could find some deserving people or deserving causes and she said she could think of one or two people she would like to have something but not the lot, and she didn't want to leave it to any charity. Then she started talking again about this woman who was killed on the road, and whom I now realise must have been your wife, Mr. Johnson, and how guilty she felt because she believed she knew who the culprit was, but she had not gone to the police."

"She did go to see my partner, though," I interrupted. "She did try to do something about it."

"I know," said Mrs. Corbett. "We had a long telephone conversation at that time too. As usual, I just listened. I knew she'd make up her own mind, whatever I said—although she might perhaps have been influenced by something I said half as a joke. This was when she rang me about ten days ago."

She paused, and I asked what it was that she had said, and for the first time she sounded a little reluctant to talk.

"I hope you will forgive me, Mr. Johnson. It really was a most unwarranted intrusion into your affairs, and my only excuse is that I was getting a little impatient with Miranda going on and on about not knowing what to do with her estate on the one hand, and worrying about your own great loss and the wicked injustice of it on the other."

"So you said, why not kill two birds with one stone and leave all her money to me," I said.

She admitted that it had been something of the sort.

I laughed. "And that's exactly what she did. It seems that I am indebted to you for my inheritance, Mrs. Corbett."

"Oh, dear. I do feel very embarrassed about it. I'm sure it must have let you in for a great deal of trouble and perhaps even unpleasantness."

"It has, rather. But it's also brought me the chance of happier things."

We talked a little longer and said we should be pleased to meet each other at Miranda's funeral. I rang off, feeling very glad that I had made this call. The art expert and Miranda's friend: two pleasant and uncomplicated people who left one with the feeling that the world was not such a bad place, after all. But they were elderly, while the unhappy Peter was young, and Grace's even more unhappy daughter had been young too. I went to bed thinking about the hopelessness of youth and the comparative contentment of age, and wondering how the one could be converted into the other.

Imogen came to me in a dream and I woke yet again to pain and loss. It will pass, I told myself; there is no need to nourish it now. And I knew then that I had finally weaned myself from the diet of grief and was ready to live as others do.

CHAPTER 10

But nevertheless Saturday is a bad day for those who live alone. All the world seems to consist of couples or families planning their week-end relaxations and festivities. I felt it again that morning and wished that I did not have to wait another twenty-four hours before seeing Grace. More and more did I long to talk to her, tell her about Peter and my thoughts about the hopelessness of the young. Her own daughter was beyond our help, but perhaps together we could think of some way to help Geoffrey's son to see a future.

The hours passed. Geoff telephoned to thank me for talking to Pete. Apparently on his return the boy had been slightly less taciturn and rather more courteous to his mother. I repeated that I would be delighted to help in any way I could. We were very formal, Geoff and I, weighed down with all that must remain unspoken between us. I longed to tell him that I did not belive Peter had killed Imogen, but I dared not. Peter had said it would only make things worse. And when I considered the complexities of guilt and distress that Geoff must have been feeling about me for many months past, I could only marvel that he had succeeded in hiding it so well. Our business partnership had certainly not suffered.

In the afternoon, I drove over to Mill Green and spent several hours at Beth's Cottage, turning out the contents of the little desk that I had promised to the young taxi-driver and looking for the cameo brooch that Rosemary Corbett had said she would like as a keepsake. I also looked in at the Plough and renewed my acquaintance with the Grants and with the farm boy Paul. There might yet be a struggle with Mervyn to face, but I had little doubt that here was to be my future home.

And Sunday I would show the house to Grace. And talk about all sorts of things, not only about Miranda and Peter. Perhaps very little about Miranda and Peter and my wife's death and her daughter's short and wretched life. Grace had not yet won through to the acceptance that I had achieved at last. There was a great bitterness and fury and despair boiling away underneath that stoical exterior, and only very gradually could it be released and dispersed. She could not stand much in the way of consolation at the moment, but she badly needed somebody who knew about it, somebody who would always just be there.

Well, here I was. And tomorrow she would be here, at Beth's Cottage, too. She hoped to be free at twelve noon but had asked me to telephone earlier in the morning to arrange when I should collect her from the hospital. Apart from a visit to Beth's Cottage, we had not yet decided how to spend the afternoon. A walk, a drive, or perhaps go over to Eastbourne or Brighton for a concert.

I awoke the next morning with a pleasurable sense of there being a good day ahead. It was raining and misty, but that didn't matter. Grace and I could entertain ourselves whatever the weather. At half past ten I rang the hospital and waited impatiently for the switchboard to locate Dr. Watson. In the end I asked to speak to Sister Jenkins. If they can't find Grace, I decided, I won't wait and try again; I'll go straight there and sit on that bench in the Out Patients Department until she's ready, and amuse myself by remembering the very different circumstances when I last sat there.

But when speech came over the wire again it was actually Grace's own voice. She sounded worried, and the Australian accent was more marked than usual.

"We've had a busy morning," she said, "with road-crash casualties."

"I'm sorry," I replied. "Does that mean you won't get off till later?"

I was disappointed, but resigned. After all, that was a doctor's life. She said she was not sure; she might perhaps be able to finish on time. Perhaps it would be best if I rang again at noon. Perhaps it would, I agreed, but this time my voice must have conveyed my dawning anxiety that something was wrong, because there was far more warmth in her voice when she replied.

"I'm truly sorry, Harry. I can't bear to think that you—"

She broke off suddenly and I heard an indrawn breath that sounded suspiciously like a struggle not to cry out.

"Grace, my dear, what is it? There's something very wrong. I'm coming round at once."

She begged me not to do that: She still had a ward round to do.

"All right, then. I'll call again in half an hour," I said, to soothe her, although in fact I had no intention of waiting so long. "I've got lots of things to tell you," I went on hastily. "You'll be delighted to hear I've taken your advice and called off my investigations. I had a talk with Peter Holdsworth that cleared it all up as far as I need to know, and that's the end of it. . . . What did you say? I'm sorry, Grace, I didn't hear you. Are you all right? Are you not well?"

I had thought my message would cheer her, but she sounded more distressed than ever.

"I'm quite all right," she replied at last. "Just rather tired. I'll have to go now, Harry. Goodbye."

"Goodbye for now. See you soon."

I doubt if she heard me. As soon as I had dropped the receiver I hurried out to the car and cursed at the Sunday tripper traffic that had come out in spite of unpromising weather and was cluttering up the road to the hospital. I don't know at what point it was that I became seriously afraid, or whether perhaps something in me had been afraid all along, ever since Grace had sat in her olive-green dress against my yellow armchair and with rigid self-control told me her story.

Don't guess, don't think at all, I said to myself as at last the cars ahead of me began to move; just get there and find her and make her finish the story, whatever it is, *whatever* it is, and never let her go again.

The main road to the coast led over the hill past

the hospital entrance. As I pulled into the outer lane
I thought: Suppose she's gone. She's running away
from me. She'll have guessed I'll be coming at once;
suppose I'm too late.

As I turned right towards the hospital gates, I
thought I saw through the corner of my eye a red
Fiat like Grace's in the line of cars travelling down
the hill. My instinct was to get back into the stream
and follow, but it would have caused a smash-up.

There was nobody at the reception desk. I ran out
into the car park again, wishing I had obeyed my instinct and driven on as soon as I got a chance instead of wasting these minutes.

Then I saw Sister Jenkins coming from the direction of the staff residence and I ran towards her.
"Dr. Watson?"

"She was called away urgently." The broad face
looked anxious. "I've never seen her like that before.
I know she's been worried to death the last couple of
days and she said she was rather expecting bad news
but she wouldn't say what. Then a phone call came
for her about twenty minutes ago and she said she'd
have to go at once and would I get someone else to
finish her rounds because she didn't know when
she'd be back."

Only with a very great effort did I manage to
speak coherently: Calmness was out of the question.

"Sister," I said, "I know what's troubling her and
I believe I can help her, but I don't know where
she's gone. Do you?"

She shook her head and then said: "Unless—"

Again I controlled myself.

"She sometimes goes to Eastbourne," said the

nurse slowly, "on some sort of family business, and always comes back upset."

Eastbourne. Where Peter's latest experiment in communal living had ended with his being charged with possessing drugs. Sedate seaside resorts do sometimes harbour such "undesirable" little communities.

"Thank you, Sister," I said. "I believe I can guess where she is. Where's the nearest telephone?"

She led me to the public call-box off the main foyer of the hospital and then said she would have to go, and I promised to let her know when I had any news of Grace.

I dialled Geoff's number. He answered himself and wanted to talk but I begged him to put Peter on at once. Thank God the boy was in.

"The address of that place you were living in at Eastbourne," I said quickly. "I've guessed the name of your friend and I need to go there."

"But I told you—they're dead!" cried Peter.

"I know. So may someone else be if you don't hurry up and tell me."

"Christ! You don't mean—!"

"Peter. Quick. Please."

He gave me a number and the name of a road and began to give directions for finding it. I cut him short. "I know it. The Beachy Head end?"

"Yes, but I don't know who'll be in the house now. It's all supposed to be broken up."

I rang off and repeated the address in my mind as I raced back to my car. The traffic had eased, but the rain had begun again and the wind was rising too. It took me half an hour to get there. I turned off from the promenade, where drivers were positioning their cars so that their passengers could stare out at a grey and increasingly angry sea; drove through quiet side roads lined with elegant villas, and finally stopped on the very outskirts of the town, not far from where a road wound up to the top of the great chalk cliff.

It was a rambling two-storey house, too big for modern needs, in quite good condition and standing in its own grounds. In driving rain I made my way over flagstones to the front door. I rang three times and banged with the knocker before anything happened. Then an upper window was opened and a woman's voice cried out angrily: "What do you want?"

"Someone who knew Adela Watson."

A gust of wind drowned my words.

"If you're press, then go away, and if you're police, we've nothing more to tell you," yelled the voice.

"I'm neither!" I shouted back. "I want to talk about Adela Watson."

"Well, I don't. Sod off."

The window was slammed shut. I banged on the door again and kept my thumb pressed to the bell. After what seemed minutes but was probably only a matter of seconds, the front door was pulled open with such a jerk that I nearly fell forwards over the step. A tallish, youngish woman stood there. Her trousers and her light blue shirt were stained and creased, but the way she stood and, above all, the way she spoke, gave her origins away. Here was the earl's daughter with a social conscience whom Geoff had mentioned.

"You run this home for drop-outs and drug addicts and you've been here two years," I said.

"Yes." It was a hiss followed by a snap.

"Adela Watson lived and died here."

"Lived here. Died elsewhere." She tried to push me out. I kept a hand and a foot inside the door.

"I'm not accusing you of anything," I said. "I admire your work for these unfortunates. All I want is to find Adela's mother. She's been here this morning to ask you something."

The surprise tactics worked. She stopped pushing at me, stood relaxed against the door, and spoke in a contemptuous voice. "If you're who I think you are, then I assure you she doesn't want to see you. I promised her I wouldn't talk to you if you turned up, but I really cannot be persecuted like this. That's the second promise I've broken this morning."

"And the first one was—?"

"Made to Pete, who blabbed it all out to me a few days ago. Adela never told me she'd run over some woman while driving without a licence. She wouldn't have told Pete if he hadn't suspected already. It was his car and she'd taken it without his permission. It wasn't fit to drive. A lethal old banger. She got it back here and crashed it against the shed round the back of the house. I scented trouble and got the boys to push it into the shed and dismantle and dispose of it bit by bit. I never asked what happened. Never knew till Peter told me. He wanted it kept quiet, but I've broken that promise by telling Adela's mother and now I've broken my promise to her by telling you. So would you please sort it all out between yourselves and leave me in peace because I have my own problems. Good morning."

She straightened up and tried to shut the door.

"Just a minute," I said, holding it open. "When did Adela's mother leave you, and where did she go?"

"She left me about ten minutes before you arrived and I presume she went back to where she works."

"How did she look? Why didn't she want me told?"

"I should think it's pretty obvious why she didn't want you told," said the disdainful voice, "and she looked as she always did after seeing Adela or speaking about her. Agonised. Pretty obvious too, I should have thought."

"Did she look as if she might be thinking of ending her own life?"

I spoke with great anger. The woman's lips parted without speech; the lofty mask looked as if it might be about to crack at last.

"There's a pretty lethal old cliff just up the road," I yelled back at her as I let go of the door and ran to my car.

She ran after me and pulled open the door of the driver's seat as I started the engine. Her eyes were twitching and her mouth was twisting. Agonised, as she might say.

"You really think—?"

"Yes, I do think it's possible. Go and alert the coastguards."

She nodded and ran back to the house.

I had wasted precious minutes, but I had gained a useful ally. She would do her best now that she was

convinced there was danger, this earl's daughter
who could shelter a girl who had killed but who
jibbed at letting the girl's mother kill herself. She
lived in the shadow of this notorious suicide spot
and would know what to do. Telephone calls were
speedier than my car grinding up the steep slope.

The wind shook the car as I came round the last of
the corners and drove along the cliff-top road, not at
great speed, because now I was up there it all seemed
unreal. My great fear had for the moment consumed
itself, and most of my mind was convinced that
Grace was by now safely back in her flat at the hospital, grieving alone, determined to avoid me because she could find no way to behave to me now
that she knew her daughter had killed my wife. How
I was to help her over this mountain I did not know,
but we would struggle along together, coping with it
as best we could.

Thus ran my thoughts while my eyes were glanc-
ing to left and right, scanning the grass bank that
went gently up from the roadway towards the edge
of the cliff, looking at the parking places where a
few determined sightseers had left their cars. Grace's
red Fiat was not among them.

She had not come up here to end her life. One moment I was sure of that. The next moment I thought:
No car, but she could have driven up the grass and
over the edge. Some people do that: Let the machine do the job. It spares them last-second uncer-
tainties on the brink; it makes doubly sure. I reached
the hotel and the coastguard station. At the latter I
could see no sign of great activity, but then, if the
lofty lady had got across her message at once, they

would have had time to get out their rescue tackle and be off on the hunt.

Which was where I ought to be myself. Fighting with the wind and the rain and searching for signs of her instead of crawling along in the car like some half-hearted tourist on the point of deciding to give up and go home on this brute of a day. I parked in the space reserved for buses and coaches and struggled up a narrow path, white chalk between the dark green of the grass either side. For a moment or two I had shelter, and then I came up to the full force of the wind and it took my breath away and I staggered to keep my balance.

I was making my way to the highest spot, where the cliff drops sheer to the rocks and sea and the lighthouse far below looks a tiny thing. Sightseers love that spot: They always gather there. But those with more desperate aims in view would choose a lonelier place, further away from the lighthouse, from the coastguards, and from the hotel.

I could not see clearly ahead. It was one of those days that had everything: driving rain, gale-force wind, and mist as well. To walk a few yards in the wrong direction was to be yet another candidate for eternity. There was nothing I could do to help. An elderly man who even in his youth never had much of a head for heights. What help could I be? And yet I had to keep moving. Ahead of me, in the mist, shapes now began to emerge and take colour. An orange raincoat, the dark blue of a police uniform. And then I heard, almost drowned by the howl of the wind, the whine of an ambulance siren, and two more uniformed figures joined the group.

I came up to the policeman, a tired-looking middle-aged sergeant who was telling people to stand back for their own safety and to give the rescue workers some more space.

"This isn't just idle curiosity," I said to him. "I have reason to be very anxious about a friend of mine. Could you tell me how matters stand?"

My voice was absolutely steady: The whole thing was quite unreal, a nightmare from which I should very soon awake.

"They've found nothing yet," replied the sergeant, "but the mist's shifting a bit now. If visibility improves they'll be able to see from the lighthouse. Did you say a friend of yours? You actually saw him go over the edge?"

"Not exactly," I said slowly, cursing myself for having let myself in for this question. The very last thing I wanted was to become bogged down in police enquiries.

"If you can help us, sir, we'd all be very grateful," continued the sergeant. "It sounded a genuine enough alarm this time, but we do get these jokers who think it's funny to—"

He broke off as a youngish man who looked like a reporter pushed himself between us. Breathing a prayer of gratitude for my escape, I left them arguing and moved behind a clump of gorse bushes, out of sight of the police sergeant, nearer to the edge of the cliff.

Suddenly I could see the whole thing in newspaper headlines: RESCUE DRAMA ON BEACHY HEAD, with a smiling photograph of the young man whose job it was to dangle at the end of a rope in atrocious

weather hundreds of feet above a raging sea, cheer-
fully risking his life to try to save those who could
not save themselves.

I wondered what he thought of it all. Did he pity
them? Did he curse them? Did it give him great satisfaction to save a life? Or was it just a job to him?

I felt sick at heart. Oh, Grace, Grace, why did you
have to do it this way? It's not like you, this great
public scene. You're quiet and reserved, and as a
doctor you should know the fatal dose to take. She
must have been distraught; a mind stretched beyond
its endurance. Her very own words when we had
talked of suicide that evening after Miranda died.
Beyond its endurance, and it was I who had driven
it there. It was my determination to discover the
truth about Imogen's death that had led to this.
When had Grace begun to suspect? Surely not at
first. Perhaps that evening when we talked so late.
And then came my phone call this morning, which
had sent her rushing to the one person who might
tell her the truth. But she could not bear the truth.
Her daughter's guilt was her own. And so she must
punish herself.

My thoughts raced round in circles. So lost was I
in this terrible pendulum swing of certainty and disbelief, hope and despair, that I did not realise I was
still moving slowly forwards. I made a great effort to
cling to the hopeful thoughts. They had found nobody yet; every minute that passed increased the
chances that Grace was still alive.

It was on a great upsurge of hope that I became
fully aware of my own movements and that I felt the
earth move beneath my feet. At the same moment

the mist around me cleared and I stared out at nothingness.

The earth moved again. Chalk crumbles easily. With the blinding clarity of total horror I felt and saw my position. What should I do? Try to step back? Cry out for help?

The rain had stopped; the wind had eased. I was standing on an incipient landslide at the very edge of the cliff. I forced myself to keep my eyes open. To shut them would be fatal. I kept looking upwards and I took deep breaths and counted them, steadying myself.

When I had counted up to ten I would, if I was still alive, try to fall backwards, absolutely flat backwards, hoping the earth behind me would hold.

I had reached six when I felt a blow on the chest that almost knocked the breath from my body. My eyes closed: I was whirling round and round as if I were in a cement-mixer. Then all of a sudden everything was still and I felt grass beneath my hand.

My first rational thought was that I had slipped down the side of the cliff and had been lucky enough to get caught on a ledge far beneath. That sometimes happened. But was I injured? Apparently not. The breathing was easy, the giddiness had gone; there was no pain. In fact it was so peaceful lying there on the soft grass that I didn't even want to open my eyes. Just let me rest.

Then I remembered Grace. I opened my eyes and blinked and heard a man's voice, rough, cheerful, satisfied.

"You've lost your bet, Bill. It wasn't a hoax. And we've caught him in time."

I sat up and stared at two sturdy young men. One of them was rolling up the rope that had been flung round me to pull me to safety.

"I'm eternally grateful to you," I said with as much firmness and dignity as I could muster, "but I assure you I had no thought of taking my own life. I just happened to go too near the edge, that's all."

"That's all, mate." The man addressed as "Bill" winked at the other as he spoke. "Just got a little too near the edge, didn't you. Never mind. No harm done. Just be more careful another time, please, sir."

"I can promise you that," I said as I got to my feet.

They rushed to assist me. I waved them aside. "I'm fine," I said. "Truly." And I began to thank them again, controlling an insane desire to laugh. Tragedy had turned to farce. The absurdity of the situation was almost more than I could bear. I felt weak and shaken, but my heart was singing. Grace was not dead: She had not thrown herself over the cliff. Finding no other victim, the rescuers had gladly seized upon myself as the reason for their search, and the man who had said it was a hoax had lost his bet.

Let it stay lost. Let them think I was the would-be suicide for whom the whole operation had been mounted. After all, they had indeed saved a life. They were content and I was content and all the rescue services would be very glad that they had not turned out in vain, and now I must get on with the job of looking for Grace.

I was just about to bid the young men goodbye

when one of them said: "Better make our report, I s'pose."

My heart sank. Of course. Officialdom had to have its reports. And the questions would take a long time; and what on earth that police sergeant would say. . . .

My mind raced. I had committed no crime. I could explain the whole thing, and when they saw my credentials they would certainly believe me. But meanwhile Grace. . . .

I simply had to get away. I couldn't possibly stay here or at the police station sorting out all this muddle. My thoughts beat around for a convincing lie.

"You'll want me to come with you," I said amicably. "Will it be in order if I just go to my car first for a moment? I've got a slightly groggy heart and I ought to be taking one of my pills."

They offered to fetch them for me. I was careful to appear to consider the offer before replying.

"That's kind of you, but it may take you time to find them, and it's really rather urgent."

We were walking along as we spoke. I could see the excitement among the little crowd of people on the cliffs. The police sergeant, followed by other uniformed men, began to walk towards us. A few yards to my right was the steep white path that led to my car. Twice the distance, to my left, lay capture.

Inspiration struck me suddenly. "Oh, my God! The press!" I cried. "Save me, you chaps. Keep 'em away. I can't face them now."

It worked. My two rescuer-guards, enticed by the prospect of seeing their pictures in the local paper, turned to face the approaching reporters. I swerved to the right, tobogganed down the chalky slope, and fell into my car. A high bank and a maze of gorse bushes concealed me from the eyes of those above.

And none of them knew the number of my car. Except the aristocratic lady, who was going to have to face all the questions. She had no love for myself, but neither did she care for the police. I would just have to pray that her natural talent for obstruction would keep me safe. She wouldn't say anything that could lead to further enquiries into her own affairs. And she did have some sort of conscience towards Grace.

Grace. Let me find her, safe, well, and willing to be comforted. After that I'll sort out all this mess and explain and apologise for as long as they want me to.

CHAPTER 11

Grace. She hadn't jumped off Beachy Head, but she could have done something else almost as drastic.

I drove at great speed. Traffic was still heading for the coast, but my side of the road was clear. My heart was racing and my breath coming in gasps. For some minutes, I wondered whether I had spoken more truly than I knew when I told the young men that I needed the heart pills in my car.

Of course there were no such pills. But there was brandy. I wasted precious minutes by the side of the road while I drank it and struggled for calm. Elderly men ought not to behave as you've been doing this morning, I said to myself: You've got to take it easier now, or you'll be no use to Grace.

I drove on more slowly, conserving my strength, and reached the hospital at two o'clock. It was with an extraordinary mixture of relief and dread and fear and hope that I asked a nurse standing near the reception desk if she knew where Dr. Watson was. The girl thought that she was off duty now, though she'd seen her earlier.

"About what time?" I asked, and waited in great anxiety for the answer.

"Oh—some time after twelve, I think."

Some time after twelve! Then she had come back

after learning the truth about her daughter. Hope came rushing in like the tide. I asked if Sister Jenkins was on duty, and on learning that she was, went straight to the ward where Miranda Porlock had died. Visiting time was just beginning; the ward sister was being questioned by various worried-looking friends and relatives of patients and I had to wait some minutes before she was free. The poor woman looked very harassed.

"Oh, Mr. Johnson," she cried. And then: "Let's go out in the corridor. It'll be more peaceful."

Oddly enough it was. People made straight for the ward, and let us alone.

"I've got a letter for you," she said, producing an envelope from her apron pocket. "Dr. Watson came back less than half an hour after you'd left here and told me she had to leave at once and wouldn't be coming back at all. I've never known such a thing! Just walking out like that at a moment's notice!"

"It's not like her," I murmured.

The nurse's fury subsided. "No, it's not. So it must be something very bad indeed. But she didn't stay to tell me what. She asked me to let Matron know and the hospital secretary so that they could get someone in to cover her work until they can make a new appointment, and of course they are all furious and are blaming me, though what on earth I had to do with it—"

She raged on for a little while and I could hardly blame her.

"Anyway, I'll have to go now. If you find out what's happened to her perhaps you'd let me know. I really liked Dr. Watson."

"Perhaps this letter will help," I said, "but I won't keep you now. Except for one thing. Did she take much luggage? She couldn't have packed up all her things, surely."

Sister Jenkins thought she had taken everything except her books and linen. That was another grievance: Please would the nurse arrange for them to be stored until Dr. Watson wrote to tell her what to do with them.

"I can help you there," I said. "I'll collect her things and store them myself. I've plenty of room."

"Oh, Mr. Johnson, that would be very kind!" Sister Jenkins became very chatty again, as people so often do when they have just said they can't possibly stay another minute. "I really can't think where Dr. Watson can have gone. Unless it's to her house—somewhere in South London. I'll give you the address. But it's let furnished for the rest of the year. And one can't simply turn tenants out, can one?"

I took the address and at last I got away. People were hovering around trying to speak to her, but she didn't seem to want to let me go. Of course she wanted me to open the letter from Grace and tell her the contents, but that I could not do. I must not read it till I was alone.

In fact I waited until I was back home. I wanted to get away from the Queen Mary Hospital as quickly as possible now that I knew Grace would return there no more. The letter was short and hastily written, but in a strong sloping hand, not the usual illegible doctor's scrawl.

"Dear Harry, Forgive me. The other night I began to suspect but this morning I've found out for sure.

You'll say it doesn't matter and we must work it through together, we who have lost our dearest ones, but I can't face you. Please try to understand. Do you know your Bible? Not the sins of the fathers, etc., but the sins of the children shall be visited upon the parent. I won't do anything drastic. I promise. But I must get away. Far away. I'll write to you. I promise that too. Thank you and forgive me. Grace."

I dropped the letter and reached for the telephone and began ringing the airports. She'd go back home, of course; to her parents who would welcome and soothe her as nobody else could at this time. I would not try to stop her, but I had to see her before she went. A letter three months hence was not the same. Our lives would have gone into very different ways by then. Here and now, in the intensity of the revelation of her daughter's guilt, I had to make her see that she had no guilt herself.

A flight to Sydney had been delayed: It would now leave at 19.30 hours. That was in four and a half hours from now, and it would take only two hours to get to Heathrow, but suddenly I knew that I could not manage the drive. Nor could I face the waiting for trains or buses. Reaction had set in. I could not rest, but my capacity for acting and deciding was almost at an end.

The answer was Country Cabs, of course. Andy Darren had told me that Sunday was one of their busiest days. I rang the number and asked for Andy himself. He'd just gone home for the rest of the day, they said. I rang his home number that he had given me and a different male voice answered—a very cultured voice. I was left on the line while an argument

took place. Poor Andy was evidently suffering a
conflict of loyalties. In the end I—and Miranda Porlock's memory and her estate—were the winners, and
a disgruntled friend was left to get his own dinner.

While I waited for Andy, I packed an overnight
bag and threw in my passport just in case; and wrote
a short note for my neighbours which I stuck to my
front door. They would all think me even more crazy
than they did already, but at least nobody need
worry about me or send out a search party. Grace
and I, what a pair we are, I thought: dropping all
our professional responsibilities at a moment's notice
and leaving other people to clear up for us. Who are
we to criticise young people like Adela and Peter?

Andy arrived and I told him enough to satisfy his
immediate curiosity and then said I must shut my
eyes and rest. I dozed and came back to full consciousness feeling very weak and giddy. Andy
handed me a thermos flask and a bar of chocolate
and bullied me into eating and drinking. I had a sudden vision of him at home: quick, neat, efficient;
unemotional but a bit of a nagger.

When we got there, he wanted to wait to bring me
home in case I didn't find my friend, but I sent him
off. If this journey proved to be in vain, then I could
go no further. There was nothing more that I could
try, and in any case I was not fit to try it. I would go
to a hotel for the night and return home tomorrow
morning to a new and different great emptiness of
life with nothing but the promise of a letter from
Australia at some distant date to keep me going.

The lounge was full of bored, impatient people,
heavy with weariness and frustration and the faint

scent of anxiety that hangs about even the most
hardened travellers. I'd given up all hope of finding
her and was becoming more and more giddy and
sick, and then suddenly there she was, right in front
of me, lying back in a chair with her eyes closed,
while a few feet away a middle-aged American couple carried on a loud and seemingly endless argument about whether or not to have anything more to
eat.

I perched on the arm of her chair and said softly:
"Grace, I had to come. I couldn't bear to let you go
without seeing you to say goodbye."

She opened her eyes, blinked, sat up, turned to
look at me, but said nothing. I gripped the arm and
the back of the chair. I was beginning to feel very ill
indeed. "Grace," I said again, and then it caught me.
The pain. In my chest and in my arm and shoulder. I
saw the compassion and the alarm in her face before
the pain swept over and drowned me.

Apparently it was only a mild heart attack. What
a bad one feels like I hate to think. After I had sat
perfectly still for some time with Grace sitting on the
arm of the chair and holding my wrist, I managed to
speak.

"What a disgusting method of preventing you
from flying away!"

She did not smile. Her face was very grave as she
questioned me. Had I ever had anything like this before? When did I last see a doctor? Etc.

When the inquisition was over, she looked a little
happier, told me she was going off to find a chem-
ist's, and strictly forbade me to try to move. The
middle-aged American couple, who had apparently

decided to postpone their eating and watch the little drama taking place near to them instead, spoke to her as she passed. I didn't catch their words, but I heard her reply.

"I am a doctor, and I'm going to get a prescription made up. He'll be all right, but he mustn't try to get up."

"We'll keep an eye on him," I heard them say.

Grace glanced back at me, and this time I did see her smile, and give a slight wink as well. I shut my eyes again and remained totally motionless, conscious all the time that I was being studied with great interest by my two guards. Just before Grace returned, their flight number was called, and another argument broke out, this time as to whether or not they could leave me. In the end, I opened my eyes and assured them that I was all right and that I would not get up, and they hurried off at last, red-faced and very agitated.

When Grace returned, I told her the thought that was uppermost in my mind: that my activities today seemed to be impinging on the lives of rather a lot of strangers. I was thinking of Beachy Head, but of course she did not know about that yet. Should I tell her? Wouldn't she be angry to learn that I had thought her capable of such an act?

She told me to shut up and swallow this.

I obeyed in both respects. "This" must have been a powerful stimulant. Before long the sickness and the dizziness and the rest of the pain had gone and I felt no worse than rather tired and weak. There was still time for her to catch her plane. I told her so.

"If you'll give me the rest of those pills and tell

me when to take them, I'm sure I can get myself to a hotel for the night and get someone to drive me home tomorrow. And I'll go straight to my doctor and follow all instructions faithfully."

She replied by holding my wrist again and putting a hand on my forehead.

"All right, then. Get up slowly," she said at last, placing an arm under my elbow. When we were standing, I said I could manage now.

She picked up my bag. "Come on. I don't know where I'm going to put you while I collect my car, but we'll find somewhere."

"Collect your car?" I echoed stupidly.

"I've paid three months' storage on it. I did mean to come back, you see."

"Then, you must go now—you must go now." I became very excited. "I can't upset your plans like this."

If someone had told me a couple of hours before that I should in all sincerity be begging Grace to leave me, I should have thought him quite mad. Yet here was I doing just that.

"Do try to keep calm, Harry," she said. "It's going to be an awful nuisance if you have another attack before we're out of here. In that case I really will have to get an ambulance and it will be hospital in London and all that that entails. I'd far rather just drive you quietly home. I think there's been more than enough misery and misunderstanding already. Don't you?"

This was exactly what I had been intending to say to her myself in my attempt to persuade her not to run away. I felt cheated, and I told her so. She laughed but said no more.

When at last we were seated in her car and crawling along in the queue making its way out of the airport, I said: "What about your luggage?"

"I couldn't get it back. I'm hoping they'll hold it someplace where I can collect it sometime next week."

I flung both arms up and leapt in my seat. "Then, you'll be staying in England!"

"Sit still, will you!" she cried. "Heart patients can't behave like that."

I sat still all the way back to Swanhurst.

Once she said as if to herself: "God knows what they'll think of me at the hospital, but they won't have made another appointment already."

Then, some time later: "Another hour to go. How do you feel, Harry?"

"Wonderful," I replied.

"That can't be true."

Of course it was not true. I was exhausted, weak, and ready to sleep round the clock. Which was no doubt what would be prescribed for me as soon as we got back to my house. But in another sense I did feel wonderful. That happy heart attack had solved it all. As the man whose wife her own daughter had killed, she could not bear to be with me. But as a human being needing her own expert care, she could not bring herself to leave me.

So let it be, I thought, so let it be. Let her fuss me and scold me and prescribe for me and make me keep still. I'll argue a bit but not too much. And by

M44

the time my convalescence is over and I am really fit
again, all will be easy between us.

We drove between the darkening hills.

"I must confess I'll be glad to be home," I said. "I
think I'll doze a little now."

"That's right," she replied. "Try to get some rest.
You'll need a lot of rest after an attack like that."

I shut my eyes and said no more. But I knew that
she was driving with very great care so as not to jerk
the car, and that every mile we covered in this way
was bringing a little bit more healing to her heart
and mind.

Anna Clarke was born in Cape Town and educated in Montreal and at Oxford. She holds degrees in both economics and English literature and has had a wide variety of jobs, mostly in publishing and university administration. She is the author of fifteen previous suspense novels, including *One of Us Must Die, Letter from the Dead, Game Set and Danger,* and *Desire to Kill.*